my husband's Wedding

STORIES BY

Patricia Watson

inanna poetry & fiction series

INANNA Publications and Education Inc.
Toronto, Canada

Copyright © 2004 Patricia Watson

No part of this book may be reproduced or transmitted in any form or by any means, electronically or mechanically, including photocopying, recording, or any information or storage retrieval system, without prior permission in writing from the publisher.

Inanna Publications and Education Inc.
operating as *Canadian Woman Studies/les cahiers de la femme*
212 Founders College, York University
4700 Keele Street
Toronto, Ontario M3J 1P3
Telephone: (416) 736-5356 Fax (416) 736-5765
Email: cws/cf@yorku.ca Web site: www.yorku.ca/cwscf

Interior design by Luciana Ricciutelli
Cover design by Valerie Fullard

Printed and bound in Canada

Library and Archives Canada Cataloguing in Publication

Watson, Patricia, 1930-
  My husband's wedding : stories / by Patricia Watson

(Inanna poetry and fiction series)
ISBN 0-9736709-0-8

I. Title. II. Series.

PS8645.A865M9 2004   C813'.6   C2004-906421-5

my husband's Wedding

The author wishes to thank Fiona Woodward as well as members of her writing group for their help and encouragement.

for Bev

Contents

Prelude
9

Who Blew Out the Candles?
15

Perfect Bliss
31

The Burial Plot
49

One Form or Another
67

Landmark Days
83

Un Bel Di…
96

Judge
114

My Husband's Wedding
126

Transitional Objects
144

Haunted Space
159

Lonely Hearts
174

Family Pictures
184

Harmony
196

Prelude

Snow is falling, blanketing the park in purest white, softening silhouettes of trees and park benches, the peaked rooftops of the Victorian houses that line the streets on either side. Street-lamps cast a warm glow; in every front window a light gleams.

The sound of bagpipes pierces the silence, and from the front door of a large house facing the park a group of adolescent girls dash to where an elderly man in kilts stands playing. He does this every year and every year the girls dance an improvised form of highland fling around him. Neighbours emerge to watch and applaud.

It's New Year's Eve, December 31, 1979. The end of one decade, the beginning of another. A block party is being held in the home of Brian and Liz Lord, a sprawling Victorian country house left over from an earlier time. 'A mother house,' Brian calls it, with doors and verandahs everywhere. Inside, he moves though the crowded living room—a tall bearded man, a William Morris look-alike—greeting old friends, welcoming young professional couples who have recently moved into the neighbourhood. 'Newcomers' Brian calls them; 'white painters' oldtimers call them.

Small children play under an enormous Christmas tree that stands at the end of the room. Around the fireplace, couples laugh and talk, sharing plans for the future, and local gossip. Two streets over, a woman has just run off with her neighbour's husband. "If they're going to behave like that," Brian quips in passing, "they should have stayed in the suburbs."

His block prides itself on being an oasis of family values, at a time when divorce rates have never been higher. A local lawyer has left his wife of twenty years for a childhood sweetheart. Founding couples of the nursery school are parting one by one. But they live on other streets.

Brian stops to talk to Tom McNally and Richard Prager. Like Brian, Richard is tall, but there the resemblance ends. He's a modest, watchful, clean-shaven man, his hair cut short. Tom is slightly shorter than either of them, but extremely handsome, with dark curly hair and a salesman's smile. They've been neighbours for twelve years.

It was Brian who discovered the neighbourhood. A city planner's dream, he called it, extolling the beauty of the park, the charm of the surrounding Victorian houses, the historic interest of the cemetery. Tom and Richard were drawn by the rock bottom prices. The street was still a slum then, several families per house, a refrigerater in every front window, a bootlegger in the middle of the block. The houses needed a lot of work, inside and out, but the gamble paid off. The neighbourhood is now one of the most fashionable in town, their houses worth a fortune.

Tom, who likes to think of himself as a smart entrepreneur, still regrets not buying up the entire block. He wanted to but Caroline put her foot down. It pains him to think he'd be a millionaire now if he'd followed his hunch. None of his other hunches have panned out. His latest, a computer business, isn't taking off the way he hoped.

Brian raises his glass. "We've a lot to celebrate. The seventies have been good to us. The eighties should be even better." The theatre he designed for an American company has just opened to great acclaim and he's been offered another contract. "Our children are healthy, our marriages thriving, our houses the envy of everyone we know."

Richard touches his glass. "I second that." A history professor, he has recently opened a bookstore, something he's dreamed of doing all his life. The Christmas sales exceeded his wildest hopes.

"I'll be right back." Tom's glass is empty.

A bar has been set up in the kitchen, where people lean against walls and counters laughing and talking. Tom helps himself to a drink—his fourth. From here he can see into the dining room where his wife Caroline, a 'pleasingly plump,' auburn-haired woman, sits at the head of the table under a cluster of balloons, helping the younger children draw up New Year's Resolutions. Little girls occupy the chairs nearest Caroline, writing diligently on the sheets of lined paper she has provided. Their brothers sprawl at the other end of the table, smirking and fidgeting, their pages blank. Sam—Liz and Brian's son—grabs his sister Katy's list, jumps up and reads aloud in a falsetto voice, "I will keep my room tidy, I will practice my piano, I will make my bed in the morning." The boys snort and guffaw, the girls murmur indignantly, looking to Caroline for help. "Give that back to Katy, this minute," she orders, then glancing up she notices Tom, glass in his hand.

Liz, Brian's wife, carries a smoked salmon from the kitchen into the living room. It lies on one of the antique blue platters she has collected over the years. She places it on the table she has draped with a white damask cloth, alongside a bone-in ham, green salad, rice salad, cheese, fruit, mincemeat tarts, and a large crimson azalea, then lights the Georgian candelabra her mother gave them as a wedding present. A small, dark-haired, pretty woman, her hair caught at the back of her neck, Liz leans across the table to adjust the angle of a serving spoon. She is wearing the low cut black gown Brian likes so much.

Brian watches, wishing they were alone. "I'm a uxorious man," he remarks to Richard.

Jo-Anne, Richard's wife, comes in from the kitchen with a tray of chutney and mustard. "I've left the hot dogs and chips for the children in the kitchen," she tells Liz. "Do you think we have enough?"

Liz laughs. "You and Caroline will have to take most of this home."

Caroline joins them. "What a feast!"

The three women have raised their children together, trading toys and baby clothes, sharing babysitters, arranging block picnics and parties like this one. All the advantages of the suburbs right downtown, Brian used to say. And like suburban wives, they have stayed home with their children. Caroline is the first to go back to work. Jo-Anne helps out in Richard's bookstore, but doesn't consider that real work. Liz, an interior decorator, does the occasional project for Brian, but one day, she promises herself, she'll study painting.

"Where are the noisemakers?" Caroline asks.

"We were going to bring some," Jo-Anne says. "I'll see if Richard has them."

The men watch Jo-Anne walk across the room. A pretty woman, Brian thinks. Delicate features, fine blond hair, a good body. Something about the way she moves reminds him of his first wife, Helen. His mind tightens with old resentment. That marriage was a disaster; this one with Liz, is forever. It's Jo-Anne's second marriage too, although Richard likes to think she was never really married before, never committed in any deep sense to her first husband. "Did you remember the noisemakers?" Jo-Anne asks Richard.

"Sorry. I've had so much on my mind."

"Don't worry. We've lots of old pots and pans." Brian says. He looks at his watch. "Time to open the champagne."

The children are assembled on the front porch, coats and hats pulled on over party clothes. Brian makes sure each child has something to rattle or bang. Richard prepares to lead them in a verse of Auld Lang Syne. The women stand in the doorway, arms crossed against the cold, smiling.

It has stopped snowing. A myriad of stars glitter overhead, a plane gliding through them. A toddler looks up and waves to the pilot.

"One minute to countdown," Brian says, raising his right hand, his eyes on his stopwatch.

The children squirm.

"Ten, nine, eight, seven, six...." Brian looks up quickly. The children freeze, as if caught moving in a game of 'Red Light, Green Light.'

"...four, three, two...."

"Happy New Year!" the children shout.

Who Blew Out the Candles?

It's a cool spring morning, the trees in leaf, tulips blooming, children on their way to school. Inside, Caroline pulls a smock over her sweater and jeans and begins to smear an old pine kitchen table with paint remover. Something she's been meaning to do for years. From the radio come the joyful sounds of a Hayden concerto. Caroline hums along, watching the paint begin to bubble. An activity she hopes will distract her from what's going on in the rest of the house.

Tom is moving out. He's rented a small apartment and has come to collect his things. Caroline has told friends on the block they decided to separate, although in fact she finally asked him to leave. In large part prompted by worry about the kids. The boys, Ian and Eric, in particular. Both bright, both doing well in school. She can't bear to think what the spectacle of their father's drinking is doing to them. Let alone their genes.

She's haunted by a TV program she saw recently in which the brain of an alcoholic was shown to be lacking in whatever it is that tells you when to stop, when you've had enough. The brain of his ten-year-old son was just the same. A predisposition, the narrator assured his audience, that needn't be fulfilled.

She hopes he's right.

Her world has been divided into drinkers and non-drinkers as long as she can remember. Her father's family was split down the middle. The men, reckless gambling drunks who didn't believe in anything.

Handsome men, like her father. The women, teetotalers—pretty women like her mother—good church-going people, pillars of society. Nobody in her mother's family ever touched a drop, not even at Christmas. They didn't keep it in the house. Nevertheless, even as a child Caroline didn't trust them. She sensed a mean-spirited, judgmental streak in most of them. They were not the kind of people who love you.

Her father was an elusive figure, coming and going at odd hours, sometimes sleeping all day long on the chesterfield, yelling at her mother. She found him scary at times, but there was the possibility of love. Even Chief—the seeing-eye dog he won in a poker game the year she turned four—thought so. A big handsome Police dog. "You take him back where you got him," her mother ordered, but her father just laughed, filling the room with the smell of stale cigar smoke and rye whisky. "Who wants to take him for a walk?"

They all did. When they reached the corner, Chief refused to cross on the red light. When it turned green, he got between them and on-coming traffic and proceeded with caution. "Watch our dog!" they shouted to kids on the street, walking back and forth across the road. "Watch our dog!"

Every night when her Dad came home Chief ran to the door to greet him. If he'd been drinking, Chief would turn and slink back to his place under the kitchen table. Which pleased Caroline's mother. But if he was sober, Chief would wag his tail, ecstatic to see him. Which her mother never was.

From the corner of her eye Caroline sees Tom and his helper shove the television from the dining room into the hallway. Turning down the radio, she hurries to them. "Please, leave that."

Tom turns and glares at her. "I'm not your father!" Then more quietly, "You can afford a new TV better than I can."

"For the kids. Just till I get a new one."

Tom's friend looks embarrassed. "Tom do you want me to start carrying out the boxes?"

"Oh, never mind." Caroline says. "Take what you want."

She walks back to the kitchen and begins to scrape the paint from the table. *I'm not your father!* Damn right. Her father had left her mother well provided for. He was a financial success once he'd stopped drinking. He would never have haggled over who got what, never expected her to feed the kids on thirty dollars a week. Why, Tom spends twice that on booze—though she has tried repeatedly to persuade him to drink less.

When her father decided to give up drinking—after his first heart attack—he checked himself into a clinic just north of Toronto. Caroline remembers it vividly. A large home built in the style of an Italian villa, furnished with antiques—the home of a wealthy stockbroker forced to flee the tax collector. A gardener looked after the grounds, a butler answered the door. "The idea," the doctor told them, "is to make the men feel good about themselves." The only women present were visiting wives and daughters. "Most alcoholics suffer from low self-esteem."

The clinic worked, but only to a point. Her father was sober long enough to establish a small business, but in less than two years he was drinking again. Caroline and her sister Barb found him—an ardent atheist when sober—crawling around the living room floor, weeping that Christ had gone from Christmas. At night they heard him screaming with D.T.s. They could remember when it took three months to reach that stage.

"Maybe it's his heart," Barb said. "Or his age," Caroline said. "We'd better take him back to the clinic.

Between them they maneuvered him into the back seat of his big black Chrysler Imperial. Their mother, Flo, climbed in beside him. Almost as soon as they were on the road, he moaned, "Oh Flo, don't ever leave me. I feel so terrible." Smiling, Flo cradled him in her arms. *He's ridiculous but he needs me,* her smile seemed to say. When he was sober, the girls knew, she wasn't so sure. He'd built his business without her, and now offered to buy her a house, a piano, anything she wanted. The prospect of happiness and ease after decades of hardship unnerved her; her role as Poor Flo was becoming untenable.

The doctor at the clinic was not pleased to see them. "You've got the wrong idea. This is not a place to dry out."

"He's in a bad way," Barb said.

"He could have another heart attack," Caroline said.

Sighing, the doctor waved them inside.

When her father checked himself out of the clinic—to keep him busy, his mind off booze—Barb and Caroline drove with him to the farmhouse where he'd been raised. It had been turned into a fishing lodge, the edge of the lake on which it stood now lined with cabins. They rented one for the weekend, bought some groceries, and settled in. Evenings they drank a lot of coffee and played a lot of cards; by day they drove around in his Chrysler, admiring the countryside. Stony fields, dotted with turn-of-the-century farmhouses, small glistening lakes ringed with wooden cottages. "God's country," he called it.

He showed them the one-room school he'd attended, the site of the wooden cabin his father—an Irish immigrant—built when he first arrived in Canada, and exactly where his mother stood the day she shot a bear from the verandah. He told them stories about his childhood, his years out west as a young man. He sang them songs, in a lilting Irish tenor. *The girl I love, Is on the magazine cover. It seems they painted her just for me...* or *If you were the only girl in the world, and I was the only boy.* Songs from when he was a young man, when he was courting Flo. Sung in a style that must have been popular then.

He took them into town for lunch, stopping to say hello to the man who ran the hardware store. "You're one of the Gibson boys!" the man exclaimed. "Well, I'll be. So what'd ya do while you were away?" You're talking about forty years, Caroline thought. "Oh, this and that," her father replied, buying gadgets he had no use for.

He was charming, he was generous. Caroline got to know him in a way that hadn't been possible in the days when he was either drinking non-stop or working non-stop to pay off his debts. His self-deprecating sense of humour surprised her most of all.

In a way she fell in love.

The day they decided to head home, he said, "You know if you girls want to give up your jobs and move back home, that's all right with me."

Meaning, I'll support you, look after you. As if he wanted them to be his children again. Well, for the first time really. At a time when most of their friends were safely married, many with children of their own.

While Caroline and Barb packed, he sat by the window drinking a final cup of coffee and stared intently at the lake, as if there lay the answer to the happiness that had eluded him, the years wasted.

Or so Caroline thought.

Back at work, he made up for lost time. Within a few years he was a comparatively wealthy man, with a large office, a devoted staff, and most important to him, more than enough in the bank to provide Flo with a good income for the rest of her life.

His second heart attack slowed him up hardly at all. "I'm not afraid of dying," he told Caroline.

When he started having pains again, the doctor warned, "If you don't take it easy, you're going to have another heart attack. Go home, go to bed, and rest." (This was before the days of heart transplants and bypass surgery.)

Home he went, but not to bed. He phoned his righthand men at the office and invited them all over for a game of poker. They played all night long, the dining room table ringed with glasses, the air thick with smoke. He didn't drink but he won, he nearly always did.

In the morning he woke Flo and told her to pack her bags, they were leaving for Florida.

"I can't possibly go this morning," she said. "I've nothing to wear...."

"Suit yourself. I'm leaving in an hour."

He walked into the bathroom, turned on the shower, and dropped dead.

It was Barb who found him.

Caroline and Barb stayed overnight with their mother. The doctor had given her something to help her sleep. Caroline and Barb sat up sharing a bottle of wine, reading aloud from e. e. cummings poem about Buffalo Bill, *Jesus he was a handsome man.*

Caroline was broken-hearted.

When the bottle was empty, Barb suggested they put his body in his Chrysler Imperial, drive down to the family farmhouse, set it in neutral, and push it into the lake.

Flo had other plans. A religious funeral, a United Church funeral. The church was full. The minister, who'd never laid eyes on him said their father was a fine man, he had surely gone to heaven. The poker players listened with straight faces then drove their cars behind the limousine provided for the family.

"I was such a bitch," Flo whimpered. A word the family had never heard her use.

No one had warned Caroline the route to the cemetery wound past her parents' apartment. For one awful moment she thought there'd been some mistake, that they were taking her father's body home again.

She closed her eyes and dug her nails into the palm of her hand while the hearse rolled by her father's bedroom window.

Within months her mother had moved to an apartment overlooking the cemetery, where she began to rethink their life together—eliminating the ugly parts, loving him in death as she'd been unable to love him when he was still alive.

If only he were still alive, Caroline thinks now, I'd be all right. But though she still dreams from time to time that he is just in hiding, her father has been dead for more than twenty years.

Tom wanders into the kitchen and checks the cupboard he used to store wine and liquor. It's empty.

"Why don't you check behind the bookcase," Caroline says drily. A cheap remark. Tom's never been a secret drinker. God, she thinks, what did I see in him? She knows the answer to that, of course. As a young woman she spent years drifting from job to job, from city to city, hoping to find someone to love, which she felt was more likely to happen far from home. She might have been drifting still but for her father's second heart attack. After that she thought she'd better stick around for a while. She landed a job in a local radio station as a production assistant and began to research and program with reckless confidence. No fear of failure; this was just something she was doing till her real life began. Her real life as wife and mother.

It was shortly after her father's funeral that Tom, who'd recently arrived from Winnipeg, came into the station to speak to her boss. "It was love at first sight," Tom liked to tell their friends. She remembers looking up from her desk, thinking, He's probably married, a man that good-looking. Movie-star handsome.

Over dinner he told her that he ran a tourist business specializing in custom designed tours, that he'd also started importing antique rugs and pottery. "One way or another," he laughed, ordering more wine, "I'm determined to make a million."

"Good luck," she smiled. "How was the move from Winnipeg?"

"Not bad at all. I'd only myself to consider."

"Your family's still in Winnipeg?"

"A brother. There's no one else."

No wife then.

He entertained her with funny stories about his work, the people he met in the rug business, in a variety of accents—English, Irish, Indian. He told her about growing up in Winnipeg—the sad details as well as the triumphs. His mother was dead, his father an alcoholic salesman.

I know you, Caroline thought. I know all about you.

They went straight to bed.

Four days later he arrived on her doorstep carrying a bottle of champagne. "Marry me," he said, leaning down to kiss her.

Would he make her happy? Would he be a good father, a good provider? Such questions never entered her mind.

You'll be all right, her son, Ian, said when Caroline told the kids Tom was leaving. It wasn't a good marriage, Lisa commented matter-of-factly. Ten-year-old Lisa. How long had she thought that? She turned to her younger son, Eric. Eric looked away. In some perverse way she felt humiliated; she'd expected the children to argue with her, to remind her of the good times. There had been good times.

The happiest, the most secure, the strongest she ever felt, was when the children were small, all tucked up in bed, their faces flushed with sleep, their small bodies trusting. Listening to Tom read to them. *Alice in Wonderland. Stuart Little. Winnie the Pooh.* Watching them open the lavish Christmas and birthday presents Tom bought for them. Sitting in the park with her neighbour Liz, watching the kids race in and out of the wading pool, screaming with pleasure. Talking about toilet training, teething, tantrums, Dr. Spock, developmental psychology, schools. Never about their husbands except in the most general way—Brian's doing this, Tom's doing that, careful to protect the privacy of their marriages.

But even then it was happiness laced with anxiety. Brian was a well-established architect, but Tom's business was a roller-coaster affair right from the start, every project a cliff-hanger. Would this idea catch on? Would the money come through in time? How long could they hold out? None of his import schemes worked. His tourist company went bankrupt. A terrible blow to Tom but a relief, in a way, to Caroline. The difference between sliding downhill and picking yourself up at the bottom, she told her sister, Barb.

Tom blamed his failures on the stinginess of Canadian consumers and, in a way, on Caroline. "Well, what do you think?" he'd ask, whether he was considering a line of Spanish clay pots or a bicycle tour along the Loire. "It sounds wonderful," she'd say. But would it sell? She didn't know.

Her father would have known.

A loud bang comes from the other part of the house. Caroline hopes it's a piece of Tom's office furniture. He'd been working from home for some time now. She was the one who'd suggested it—after his company went bankrupt. "Just for a while. Just till things get going again."

Brian had helped Tom make the move. They rented a U-Haul and took the boys with them to carry small things. Caroline fixed coffee and poured soft drinks for the boys. What had started out as a really depressing day turned almost festive. The men moved the sofa and television into the dining room and set up Tom's desk, filing cabinet, and leather chairs in the living room, a high-ceilinged Victorian room with built-in bookshelves and a fireplace. When everything was in place, Tom brightened considerably.

"A very respectable office," Brian said.

"It is, isn't it? How about a drink?"

"Too early for me. I should see if Liz needs help."

"Well, I really appreciate......" Tom began.

"Nonsense," Brian said. "That's what neighbours are for."

Tom poured himself a stiff one. "I met a really interesting guy last night," he told Caroline. "He wants to start a computer business."

"Tom, you don't know anything about computers."

"That's where the money is. Any fool knows that."

He drinks too much, she thought. Not as much as her father did, but too much. Tom drank Scotch while she cooked dinner, then over dinner they shared a bottle of wine. After dinner Tom switched back to Scotch, leaving whatever was left of the wine to her.

Her father would have been in seventh heaven; her mother never drank with him, ever.

In the early years of their marriage, drinking had seemed sexy, even daring, to Caroline. Once a week, whether they were overdrawn at the bank or not, Tom would arrive home with a cartonful of assorted wines. Expensive wines. (Her father never drank wine. Whisky, beer, but never wine.) "I got us a treat," he'd smile, as if this was an exception, not the rule. In time she began to think it would be a treat not to have a bottle of wine with dinner. She began to feel like an actress sitting next to Tom, glass in hand, pretending to watch the eleven o'clock news.

"I think I'll go to bed now," she'd say, groggy with sleep and too much wine.

"I'll be up in a minute," he'd say.

From upstairs she'd hear the music start. Surging, romantic music played at top volume. Beethoven or Brahms. Her father used to play old Bing Crosby records, Mark, Kenny, the Mills Brothers.

> *If I had my way dear, forever there'd be,*
> *A garden of roses for you and for me,*
> *A thousand and one things dear I would do,*
> *Just for you, just for you, just for you…*

She'd wake in the middle of the night, Tom's side of the bed empty. Downstairs she'd find him asleep on the sofa, all the lights on, the needle sliding back and forth across the record.

Their sex life became erratic. When they did make love—often first thing in the morning, both a little hungover—it could still be wonderful. The pleasure and release, that sweet, safe place they reached together. But then, as if he couldn't bear such closeness or she didn't deserve such pleasure, Tom would withdraw into his world of work and worry and she'd be left feeling as if she'd just made love on the edge of a cliff.

She began to hoard, to squirrel away as much cash as possible, to buy clothes for the children and herself at the Crippled Civilians. The week Tom came home wearing a new, six hundred dollar raincoat, she searched the stores until she found a fifty dollar raincoat for herself. She began to re-dye her washables for longer life. "You're becoming eccentric," Barb told her. Caroline felt she had no choice.

One night Tom sat bolt upright in bed beside her. "I'm never going to be rich," he said. "I'm never going to make a million."

She glanced at the clock: it was after three. "Tom," she said impatiently, "It doesn't matter."

"You castrating bitch," he said, turning his back on her.

The morning Tom's application for a loan was turned down by the bank, Caroline thought, Now he'll get a job, a real job, with a real salary. But he spent the afternoon drawing up a household budget that included holidays in the Bahamas, weekly movies, subscriptions to glossy magazines, the latest books, records, VCR equipment, at-home parties every Sunday, a cleaning woman two days a week. He added it up and showed it to Caroline. "There, that's how much we've got to earn, he said, his confidence in himself and their future restored. "Do I have time for another drink before dinner?"

Caroline smiled the way her mother used to smile when the bailiffs came to the door. We're never going to lead a normal life, she thought. Like Brian and Liz. We're never going to be financially secure. Her father had made a small fortune when he finally gave up drinking, but she could no longer delude herself that Tom would do the same.

Tom's mood rose and fell with his financial prospects. Caroline never knew who to expect at the end of the day—the exuberant, funny, cocky entrepreneur she'd fallen in love with, or the solemn, suffering St. Sebastian of import-export, ready for a drink.

The night he told her he'd decided to go ahead with the computer scheme, he'd find the money somehow, she said she was going to get a job. "Just till things get going." A friend of Brian's had started a small film company; they needed a Girl Friday, someone to manage the office, answer the phone, do odd jobs. Brian had said he'd put in a good word for her.

"Suit yourself." Tom tilted the wine bottle toward her glass.

Caroline shook her head. "I won't have anymore." From now on she'd drink only as much as she wanted.

With her first paycheque, she took Tom and the children to a neighbourhood restaurant for dinner. "What would you like to drink?" she smiled. Tom ordered a double martini, an expensive bottle of wine, and brandy with coffee. But not even this could dampen her spirits. The waiting was over, the disappointments were over, she was in charge of her life. For the first time in years she could stop worrying about money; she knew how much she was earning, how much she owed, and would try to balance the two. Her idea of a budget.

Tom was out of town trying to line up investors the day she got her promotion. Her boss had sent her out to interview three retired men about their hobbies—genealogy, bonsai gardening, and weaving—and was very pleased with her report. "First rate," he said.

"Beginner's luck," she said.

"No, you've got a real flair. We'll get someone else to answer the phone."

She bought a bottle of champagne on the way home and invited Liz and Brian to share it.

"I'm not surprised," Brian said. "You're a very intelligent woman." He raised his glass. "I predict your career is going to take off like a rocket."

It's just as well Tom isn't here, Caroline thought.

She had begun research for a film about women and ageing when Tom walked in.

"We've got to talk," he said.

"Tom, I'm on the phone."

"Dr. Robertson's had a cancellation," the voice on the other end of the line told Caroline. "She can see you this morning at ten."

"Great. I'll be there." Dr. Robertson, a well-known feminine psychiatrist, was her last hope. She had interviewed a psychiatrist called Dr. Lucas, but he knew nothing about the menopausal years and suggested she talk to Dr. James, a colleague at the Clarke Institute. But as it turned out, psychiatry for Dr. James ended with the last period. He had never wondered how women feel after that.

Caroline poured two cups of coffee, added milk and sugar to Tom's, and carried them into the living room. "I've got a ten o'clock appointment," she said.

"I don't care what time your appointment is. You haven't done any of the things you agreed to do."

What things, she wondered. What have I done now, or not

done. Tidied the spice rack? He's punishing me.

"Women in their forties and fifties can be very, very powerful," Dr. Robertson said. Caroline guessed she was in her early sixties, it was hard to tell.

"If women have been home with children, and their careers are just starting, they're on an up escalator, while their husbands may be on the way down, over the hill, or looking at it. It makes them very nervous."

That rang a bell.

"The male ego is very fragile," Dr. Robertson continued.

"But why? They have all the privileges."

"They don't feel they have the same right to be here that we have. The same biological right. Every woman who has given birth knows that she alone could have produced that particular child. Her existence is justified. A man doesn't feel that. They're afraid we're laughing at them."

If Tom came home and found her laughing and talking with Liz and Jo-Anne, Caroline knew he'd be very uncomfortable. Unless of course the kids were with them.

"But laughing at what?"

"The size of their penises," Dr. Robertson said, and they both laughed.

"We don't want to listen to their old stories one more time," she continued. "So they may look around for someone younger, someone who hasn't heard their stories before."

Tom has never been unfaithful to me, Caroline thought.

On the way home she picked up two steaks and a bottle of red wine. Tom's favourite meal. She hadn't cooked anything special in ages. She fed the kids early then set the table for two in the dining room, put a log in the fireplace, and waited.

But Tom didn't come home for dinner. It was after nine o'clock when he finally arrived. "I think we should have some time apart," he said.

Caroline could tell he'd been drinking.

"I'll move into Neil's."

His brother, Neil. How long would Neil put up with him?

The next weekend Tom came to pick up the kids. Neil had gone away for a few days, he told her, so there was room for them to stay. "I'll bring them back in time for school." Caroline stood on the verandah and watched them drive off.

For the first time in almost twenty years she was completely alone. During the day she enjoyed the sense of freedom, but at night she lay in bed listening for footsteps on the stairs. What if someone broke into the house? Face it, she told herself impatiently, what do you have to fear? What's the worst that could happen? The worst she could imagine was a young man, knife in hand, creeping up the stairs, his face hidden by shadows.

Maybe she should get a dog for times like this. A German Shepherd. A police dog like Chief, the one her father won at poker. How he'd loved that dog. She thinks of the year Chief developed distemper. Her father had looked after him, carrying him up and down the basement stairs all winter long, giving him his medicine. By spring Chief was better, but his coat had lost its sheen and he shuffled when he walked. "His nerves are bad," their mother warned them.

Once when her mother raised her hand, Chief got between her and Caroline, baring his teeth. Another time he stood guard as Caroline tried to ride her new red tricycle on the sidewalk outside their house. An old man came along, put out his hand to give her a push, and Chief bit right through his wrist.

He had to be put down. Her father took him to the Humane Society. As Chief was led away, her father told them later, he turned and looked back—sad, knowing.

Tom was back in a couple of weeks. He would sleep on the couch, he told her, until he found a place of his own. He packed his records in a box, opened the newspaper, and began to circle the want-ads.

Caroline couldn't bear the thought of his living in some tacky bachelor apartment, all alone. She wanted to divide herself in two: to look after Tom as she had wanted to look after her father, every man she'd every loved, and still get on with her life. This is Tom's home, she thought, we are a family, there must be something we can do to make it work. She got the name of a marriage counselor. "Perhaps you can both tell me in your words what you think is wrong with your marriage," he said. Tom said he would go first. By the time he'd finished telling Dr. Irving all that was wrong with Caroline, the hour was up. What was worse, Dr. Irving seemed to sympathize. "I certainly wouldn't want to have to worry about housework," he said. "I leave those things up to my wife."

Not a word about work, finances, drinking.

On the way home Tom stopped at the local wine store and bought a carton of expensive red, which he carried into the house and stored in the kitchen cupboard. But then almost immediately he opened the cupboard door and removed a bottle. "Want a glass?" Caroline shook her head. He shrugged, as if to say, Suit yourself. He carried the bottle and a glass into the living room—whether to relax or celebrate Caroline wasn't sure—and within moments the house was filled with the sound of his favourite Beethoven symphony. By the time the children came bursting in the front door from school, laughing and talking, he had dozed off on the chesterfield and the bottle was almost empty.

As soon as they saw him, the children were silent. Eric shrugged, as if to say, So what else is new?

That night Caroline dreamt Flo and Barb had come to tell her that her father was dead.

"How shall I mourn him?" she asked, hurrying along beside them toward the corner store.

"Look back," her mother said, looking over her own shoulder as if to demonstrate how it was done. "Look back."

Caroline did what she was told, and she tried to feel sad. But in her dream she couldn't remember what her father looked like—it seemed such a long time since she'd lost him.

Outside a door slams. Caroline hears a muffled shout. It's over, she thinks. She waits a moment to be sure, then walks through the house noting what's missing: Tom's desk, his filing cabinets, a carpet, a wingchair, a couch, a few pictures, a table and a couple of dining room chairs. And a plant. That surprises her.

He has left the television.

She looks out the window of the front door. The truck is gone, but Tom is sitting on a park bench across the way, looking back at the house.

A forlorn, lonely figure.

How long will I feel guilty? She wonders. She wants to weep, whether for Tom or her father she's not sure.

Her mother, she knows, still tends her father's grave. Recently Flo had arrived for dinner dressed in her Sunday best. Soft blue woolen dress, a paisley scarf, pillbox hat. Barb's youngest—little Susie, a solemn child—asked where she had been. "You look so nice, Grandma."

"I've been to the cemetery, Susie," Flo said. "It's your grandfather's birthday today."

There was a moment of puzzled silence before Susie, who had just celebrated her fifth birthday, asked, "Who blew out the candles?"

Perfect Bliss

The spring she and Tom called it quits, Caroline flew to Rome with her old friend Molly. The trip was Molly's idea. "There are certain kinds of pain that don't travel," she said. Molly had been through a divorce or two herself.

On the plane Molly made Caroline swear there would be no talk of husbands or children in Rome, so once they had checked into their hotel—a small pensione near the Piazza di Spagna—they climbed the Spanish steps, paused in front of the house where Keats died, admired the garden of the Villa Medici, then ordered lunch in the local trattoria and began to swap stories from their childhood. Molly had almost perfect recall from the age of three. Caroline's memories were like lights turned on and and off in the dark. She could remember the year she turned five, but nothing from six to eight, the year she turned nine, then very little until she turned fourteen, the year she met Molly, the year her family moved to Queen's Corners.

Her mother told her they were moving the last day of school. "I got my report card, I passed," Caroline said, closing the door behind her. She was pleased. She'd done well in all subjects, especially algebra—an A, the only one in her class. "An industrious student with an insatiable need to make things turn out right," her teacher had written on her report card.

"Put it on the mantelpiece," her mother said. " I'll look at it later." She was emptying the contents of the hall table into a carton. Family photographs, black and white snaps, some of them cracked, here and there a corner missing. Everybody stood facing the camera, smiling. No close-ups. A photographer's portrait of her brother Jim as a baby, small legs encased in braces. Herself and Barb sitting on a pony outside the house on Elm Street. Margaret looking like a movie star at age sixteen.

"Why are you doing that?"

"We're moving."

"Moving?"

"Your grandfather found us a place in Queen's Corners."

"We can't move," Caroline protested. "Not again, not now." Now that she knew everbody, now that she was having fun. And not to the country, not to where her grandfather lived.

"You'll have to help me pack."

"I don't *want* to move."

"We can't afford this place any longer," her mother said with a how-can-you-be-so-selfish-at-a-time-like-this look. "You should be grateful we'll have a roof over our heads."

"I *won't* move." Caroline crumpled her report card, threw it in the fireplace and ran upstairs, thinking how much she hated her mother. These days, she usually hated her father. It was his fault they were always moving. This time because he had joined the navy. Usually it was because of his drinking. Once he started, he'd be drunk till the landlord kicked them out.

In her room, Caroline threw herself face down on the bed. She loved this house. It was a mansion compared to the last place they lived, all eight of them crowded into a few rooms in a slummy part of town. That was the worst, this was the biggest and the best. It had an attic, a pantry, a sunroom, six bedrooms, and three fireplaces. Her father could make a lot of money if he put his mind to it. Even when other men were out of work. He was a salesman, a good one. People liked him, they said he was a handsome man.

Her mother said he was two-faced, that when he smiled and talked to the neighbours in that friendly way, it was all a big act. Caroline didn't blame her. One minute he'd be on the back porch telling the man next door his garden looked wonderful, the next minute he'd be in the kitchen taking money from her purse.

Once Caroline was in the kitchen when he came looking for it. "Where's your purse," he demanded. She could see it hanging on the back of the door. Her mother motioned for her to grab it. Caroline got it, but he yanked it from her hand.

"Bastard!" she yelled at him.

"I'll deal with you later, young lady," he said quietly, then opened the purse, took what money there was and slammed out of the house.

"Don't worry," her mother said. "He'll forget all about it."

But when he returned, he said he expected an apology from Caroline. Never, she thought. He took off his belt. Never. The first blow landed on the back of her legs. It hurt, but she expected that. What she didn't expect was her mother to start crying. "Please, Caroline," she snivelled, "apologize to your father. Please."

Caroline was furious. I'm standing up to him, she thought. Why can't she?

Another blow landed. And another. Until welts began to stand out on her legs. He stopped then, giving her mother an accusing look, as if she were to blame, and left.

"Oh Caroline," her mother wept.

"Don't say anything more," Caroline said angrily.

Outside she sat on the back porch. The sun on her legs felt good. She'd sit there till her brothers came home from work and show them her wounds. In a way she was prouder of them than she was of her A in algebra.

Well, now her father was gone. Caroline sat up and opened her bedroom window so she could listen to the train passing a couple of blocks away. She loved this room. It was the first one she'd ever had of her own. It was small but there was a fireplace with bookshelves on either side. It was supposed to be a den, her mother had told her. On Saturdays Caroline liked to lie in bed reading, *Gone With The Wind* or *For Whom The Bell Tolls*. Books from the library. She used the bookshelves for her clothes and scrapbooks. Scrapbooks filled with full-page colour photographs of movie stars. Jean Pierre Aumont, Robert Stack, Walter Pidgeon. Handsome men with even teeth and curly hair.

Now she'd have to pack all her scrapbooks. In what? She had hoped with so much space her parents would stop fighting, but whether her father was drunk or sober, her mother was furious at him. The moment he came through the door she'd start. "I don't have to ask where you've been."

"Where's my supper?"

"You think I'm going make you supper at this hour of the night?"

"Flo, I'll give you five minutes to get up off that chair."

Caroline and her brothers and sisters would lie in bed listening, waiting. One night Flo came flying up the stairs into Caroline's room. He was right behind her, ordering her across the hall. Caroline's brothers ran in after them. Her mother started crying, her father yelling, her brothers shouting, "Don't you touch her."

But in the end she did what he wanted. She preceded him across the hall to their bedroom—her head high, back straight as an arrow. He slammed the door behind them.

Caroline huddled with her brothers in the sudden calm. Nobody said a word about what was going on behind the door. Her brothers talked about what they would like to do to him some day. Caroline wondered why, if Flo was going to give in anyway, she hadn't just made him supper so the rest of them could sleep. Why she never had a drink with him like some of the other mothers did. Why, for that matter, she didn't leave him.

It was shortly after this that her father joined the navy. They gave him a uniform and off he went to Halifax. It wasn't the first time he'd left, but it was the first time they knew where he was going. Her mother hugged him goodbye with tears in her eyes. Tears.

Caroline reached for one of her scrapbooks. It opened at a picture of Jean-Pierre Aumont. She'd seen him in "Assignment in Brittany" three times. He was a secret agent assigned to a small French fishing village occupied by the Nazis. He fell in love with Susan Peters and Susan Peters fell in love with him. It was all so hopeless. So hopeless and romantic and sad and dangerous.

Caroline closed the book. She would not move to the country. She'd quit school and get a job like Jean, the redhead who lived over the drugstore. Jean worked in an office downtown somewhere and, as far as Caroline could tell, had everything anyone needed to be happy: tweed jackets, pleated skirts, turtleneck sweaters; pancake makeup, lipstick, silk stockings. Jean was eighteen but everybody said she looked older.

Caroline walked into the bathroom and stared at herself in the mirror. How old did she look? Fifteen? She undid her ponytail, letting her hair fall around her shoulders. Maybe sixteen. Certainly not fourteen.

Caroline found her mother in the living room, sorting through Jim's records. Cowboy songs, Ink Spots, Bing Crosby, Mills Brothers. Jim loved music. Someone had given him a guitar when he turned ten—because he was crippled, Caroline supposed—and he played it by the hour and sang. They all sang. Jim had a good baritone voice. Barb sang alto. Al sang tenor and Caroline sang melody with Jim. Cowboy songs, or Mills Brothers favourites in three part harmony.

"I'm going to quit school, and get a job."

Her mother didn't look up. "You can quit school when you're sixteen. Not before."

"I'm not going to Queen's Corners."

Her mother didn't let on she'd heard.

Caroline went outside and sat on the front porch. Jerry, the boy next door, was getting on his bike. "Hey Carlie, aren't you coming?"

The kids in the neighbourhood rode their bikes up and down the streets, in and out of the park, as long as the daylight lasted. When the streetlights came on, they'd lean on their handlebars and tell each other the latest. Caroline loved these evenings, but it wouldn't be the same now that she was leaving.

"No, I've got things to do."

She decided to walk over and see if Jean was home from work. She hurried to the corner then sauntered along Springhill towards the drugstore, thinking about Jean. The way she checked that the seams of her stocking were straight, then puffed up her pompadour. The way she put her lipstick on: one coat, a dab of powder to make it stick, then a second coat. She did it with such sureness, such skill, letting nothing distract her. "There," she'd say, turning from the mirror to smile at Caroline, "that will last for hours." As if nothing more was needed to meet life's ups and downs. What Caroline admired most about Jean, she thought now, were her new false teeth, pearly white and even in a way her own would never be.

She rang the bell and waited. When no one answered, she asked the man in the drugstore if he'd seen Jean. He said he thought she'd gone out of town for a couple of weeks.

"A couple of weeks?" They'd be gone before Jean got back.

Caroline sat in the back seat with her two younger sisters, the dog and the cat, feeling all alone in an unjust world. Her mother sat in the front seat next to her grandfather, who'd come down to drive them to the country. The neighbours rushed over to say goodbye to Flo. "I'm so sad to be leaving," she told them, tears in her eyes. They shook their heads in sympathy. "Take good care of poor Flo," they admonished Caroline.

That was what they called her mother, poor Flo.

Her brothers were lucky; they had rented a room and were staying in the city. Her eldest sister was married with a baby and a place of her own, so except on weekends there would just be the four of them in the new house. Her mother, her two younger sisters and her. Caroline hoped it wasn't some terrible dump.

She hadn't been to Queen's Corners since her grandmother's funeral, but she recognized the church steeple as soon as it loomed in the distance. A red brick church with a cemetery on one side, the minister's house on the other. From the church it was only a few minutes to the main intersection. A general store on one corner, on another a garage where old men in overalls gathered to talk. On the third, a large house hidden by a high cedar hedge, on the fourth nothing except an unused pasture overgrown with wild grass and weeds. Her grandfather's house was one of about a dozen houses strung along the main road in either direction. That was all. Not a drugstore. Not even a school.

"There's a school bus that'll take you to the high school in Carlton Hill," her grandfather said, as if reading her thoughts. "Your house is over there," he added, waving vaguely in the direction of the pasture. He turned right, drove the length of the pasture, turned right again onto a dirt road and stopped in front of a small white frame house. The front verandah sloped to one side, the paint was peeling. If any of my friends in the city saw this, Caroline thought, I'd die.

The inside was worse. There was an ugly black stove in the living room and in the kitchen, a bathtub with claw feet and copper lining. But no sink, no running water. There was an outhouse at the end of the garden. They were going to have to go outside. Like animals.

Upstairs were three bedrooms. A big one with two small ones off to the side. No hallway. Flo said Caroline could have her pick of the two smaller rooms, her two younger sisters would share the other. Caroline chose the one closest to the stairs, and leaned out the window. Nothing to see. Just the pasture and the outhouse.

Everyone in Queen's Corners could see the outhouse.

Dear Diary, I hate the country. I hate this house.

"Carlie?" her mother called. "There's someone to see you."

Reluctantly Caroline closed her diary and slipped it under her pillow. Downstairs a girl her age, plump with long braids and pimples on her forehead, stood in the living room, smiling. She said her name was Marg Loughheed. Her father owned the pasture next door and her uncle drove the bus that would take them to high school in the fall. He also drove to town every Saturday morning to the farmers' market. Caroline brightened, thinking Marg was going to suggest they go to town with him, but no, she wanted to know if Caroline would like to go to Sunday School with her.

Caroline knew that would please her mother. Whenever they moved to a new neighbourhood, Flo would make an effort to send them to Sunday School. Which wasn't easy, with six kids and no money for clothes, let alone extras like hats and gloves. There were times when Caroline and her sister Barb each had to wear one white glove and carry one white sock, to create the illusion of a pair. "No one will know the difference," Flo would tell them. But *they* knew, they didn't want to go.

Caroline didn't want to go now, but it occurred to her that Sunday School might be the only place in Queen's Corners to meet anyone. "I'll try anything once," she said to Marg, with what she hoped was a worldly smile.

Sunday morning Marg called for her at a quarter to eleven and they walked down the road together. No sidewalks, just a path through sandy grass and a ditch by the side of the road. Here and there clumps of chicory growing straight up into the sun. Nothing to look at but fields and houses set back from the road. Unfriendly, watchful houses, it seemed to Caroline. A few cars passed them on their way to church.

Marg led the way down into the church basement and introduced Caroline to her Sunday School class. Three boys and five girls sitting in a circle, the girls wearing hats, the boys in long pants. Boys with close-set eyes, straight brown hair and big teeth. Brothers or cousins, Caroline supposed, disliking them on sight. They nodded, unsmiling. Miss Stibbard, the Sunday School teacher, was pretty in a country sort of way. She wore a sky blue dress and a straw hat covered with flowers, in her hand a small black bible.

It was Temperance Week, she reminded them, pointing to the pledge she had pinned to the bulletin board. "I expect all of you to sign it." A form of insurance, she said, against the evils drink could lead to—drunkenness, gambling, swearing, fighting, poverty, sin. Playing cards on Sunday was a sin, so was dancing.

Marg put up her hand. "If a beer truck drives by my house," she said. "I pray it'll roll over and the driver'll be killed."

Caroline's face burned. People talk in the country, her mother had warned her. They have nothing else to do. Her father hadn't had a single drink since he joined the navy, but Caroline suspected Queen's Corners knew all about his past record.

"A social drink now and then never hurt anybody," she said, trying to sound casual, sophisticated, like someone from the city should. "You just have to know when to stop. To exercise control."

There was a moment of shocked silence, as if the devil himself had joined the class.

They're nothing but a bunch of hicks, Caroline thought.

"Well," Miss Stibbard said. "That might well be. But most of us in Queen's Corners think it's easier and wiser not to start."

Caroline was the only one who remained seated when it was time to sign the pledge. She knew she wouldn't be asked back, that she'd spend the rest of the summer alone.

Her father had written he was coming home on leave. He arrived the following Saturday, at six in the morning, pounding on the door to wake them. "I'll see who it is," her mother said, hurrying downstairs. "It's you!" Caroline heard her cry. She couldn't make out what her father said but she distinctly heard her mother laugh and say in a low, musical voice Caroline had never heard before, "Wouldn't you know, I got my period."

Caroline was stunned. As if without it they might have gone to bed without a fight. As if....

"Girls, come down," her mother called up the stairs. "It's your father."

He was sitting at the kitchen table. He'd hung his uniform jacket over the back of his chair. The sleeves of his white shirt were rolled to the elbow, the legs of his dark serge trousers crossed beneath the table. He seemed like a stranger.

Flo was making him breakfast—bacon and eggs—talking to

him like he was someone she'd just met. How was your trip? You must be exhausted. Caroline watched, amazed, as she placed two slices of tomato on a plate next to the bacon, then put the plate on the table in front of him. Would he like some marmalade with his toast? Another cup of coffee?

He picked up his fork, smiled, "This looks wonderful." He noticed Caroline. "Well young lady, how do you like Queen's Corners?"

"It's all right, I guess." Her mother had warned them not to bother their father about anything—this might be his only visit home before going overseas.

"The country air will do you good."

After breakfast he changed into his old clothes and cut the lawn, whistling as he worked. Then he got the car out, washed and polished it, and took them for a ride over the back roads. He stopped at the top of a hill so Flo could admire the view—green pasture, a few cows grazing, a stream overhung with willows. He leaned his elbow on the window and talked to them about Halifax—the harbour, the open sea, the ships that came and went—as if that was where he was from.

Over dinner he told them about life at the base. What time they got up, when they had lunch, what they did all day long. "The young men at the base call me 'Pops'," he laughed.

Caroline felt a sudden stab of sadness. The men at the base knew her father in a way she never would. He'd found happiness in the disciplined world of men, away from her mother, her sisters and herself. He probably wishes he were there now, she thought.

"I think I'll wander up to the store," he said," and get a pack of cigarettes while the girls tidy up."

"You go with him," Flo whispered to Caroline.

Caroline knew what she was thinking: he'd ask one of the men at the garage the way to the nearest bootlegger. She pictured him—drunk in his uniform—staggering past the general store while Marg Lougheed stood in the middle of the pasture praying he'd be run over by a speeding car.

"Dad, I'll come with you."

"No, you stay and help your mother with the dishes."

The screen door slammed behind him. They hurried to the window and watched as he walked along the sideroad towards the intersection. He paused in front of the garage, said a few words to the old men in overalls, then crossed to the general store and went in. He came out carrying a large brown paper bag and headed home.

"What did you get?" Flo asked, trying to hide her apprehension.

"Some ice-cream for you and the girls." He put a large carton of Neapoliton on the table. "Some cigarettes for me. And a couple of decks of cards. I'm going to teach you how to play progressive rummy. The game we play at the base."

Caroline had never seen her parents play before. Flo laid down her cards as fast as she could, afraid of getting caught. Her father held his until the very last minute, then, laughing, laid them down in one fell swoop, catching everybody.

The next morning, he pressed his uniform with a wet tea towel on the kitchen table, filling the room with the smell of damp wool. A smell that would remind Caroline of him for the rest of her life. He polished the brass buttons on his jacket and buffed his shoes, already talking about when he'd have to leave. As soon as he was dressed, he called them outside and took snapshots to take back to the base. One shot of the girls standing in a row, their arms around one another, smiling. One of Barb standing at attention, wearing his navy hat. Caroline holding the cat. The dog sleeping. Flo, in her apron, standing by the kitchen door. Then Flo took one of him wearing his hat, another of him standing with the girls. No one thought to take a picture of the two of them together.

And then he was gone.

"We might never see him again," Flo said, when the taxi was out of sight.

Caroline spent whole days lying in bed, reading books she'd found in her grandfather's house: *The Girl of the Limberlost*, a Thomas

Hardy novel, a collection of the plays by Shakespeare.

"Get out of bed," her mother pleaded.

"There's nothing to do."

"Go for a walk."

"There's nothing to look at."

"There's a swimming hole down the sideroad under the bridge. I want you to go and take your sisters with you."

"No." Caroline kept her eyes on her book.

"Caroline you love to swim."

"In a swimming pool."

"You can't just lie there day after day."

"It wasn't my idea to move here." Caroline sat up. "I'm going to phone Aunt Alice and see if I can stay with her for the summer."

Saturday morning Caroline got a lift to town with Marg Lougheed's uncle. He was waiting in his truck outside the garage. Wordlessly he leaned over and opened the door of the cab. Caroline stepped up and in, stashing her small suitcase at her feet. It was five o'clock in the morning, there wasn't another soul in sight.

"So you're Barney Henderson's granddaughter," he said, setting the truck in motion. He was a tall, thin, colourless man, in overalls and an old brown fedora. So thin his overalls stood out a few inches from his chest.

Caroline nodded.

"I suppose you'll be going to the high school come fall."

"Yes." She'd been awake most of the night, afraid she wouldn't hear the alarm clock. She leaned against the seat and closed her eyes. Marg's uncle woke her when they reached the city. "We're here," he said, pulling over to the curb. The sun was high in the sky and a streetcar was clanging towards them, past a row of small shops where shopkeepers were piling fruit and vegetables into the bins on the sidewalk. Caroline grabbed her small suitcase, thanked Marg's uncle, and ran for the streetcar, exulting in the noise, exulting in the smell of the city, the feel of the pavement under her feet.

Aunt Alice lived in a little house, one of a row of semi-detached houses that stretched as far as the eye could see. A tidy, cosy, orderly house, like Aunt Alice herself. It was always the same: the sound of the clock on the mantel ticking, an eiderdown at the foot of each bed, breakfast with lots of bacon every day in the big sunny kitchen. In the corner of the dining room, the upright piano on which Caroline had taught herself to play La Paloma, picking out the notes one by one.

At a quarter to nine, Caroline walked to the neighbourhood Woolworth's and asked to speak to the manager. Mr. Taylor was a short plump man with a slick of black hair and light blue eyes. He wore a tight brown suit and held a pipe in his hand. "You're in luck," he smiled. "We need help on the hardware counter, you can start right away. I'll introduce you to Ethel, she's in charge of hardware."

Ethel was a tiny woman with bow-legs and very little chin. She was dressed like an old person, her hair pulled back in a bun, though Caroline guessed she couldn't be more than twenty-five. She didn't seem too pleased with Caroline. Caroline didn't care. She loved the store, loved being there before any of the customers. She helped Ethel fill the counter with nuts and bolts, light bulbs and glass cutters, listening to the girls on the next counter talk about their boyfriends. "Keep your hands to yourself, I told him. 'Just a look,' he said, 'I won't do anything.' Nothing doing, I said."

Mr. Taylor strolled up and down, checking everything was in order. He paused by their counter to light his pipe. "It's a beautiful day," he said. "Go on, look out the window, look up at the sky. Is the sun shining? Are there clouds up there? Each day is special, a gift in itself. No two days are alike."

He's right, Caroline thought. No two days *are* alike.

Ethel told her to take her coffee break with Molly, the girl on cosmetics. Molly had bright red hair. "I'm sixteen," she told Caroline. "Still in school. This is just a summer job." She'd been smoking for over a year, she didn't have a boyfriend, but she went to CYO dances every Wednesday night. CYO stood for the

Catholic Youth Organization, though nobody called it that. She considered herself lucky to be working on the cosmetics counter. "Too bad you got stuck with Ethel on the hardware counter."

She studied Caroline for a moment. "You know with a little make-up you could look really glamourous," she said. "You've got good bone structure and colouring, but your eyebrows are your best feature. Women pay a lot of money to have their eyebrows arched like that."

Saturday, Molly invited Caroline to sleep over at her place, a house almost identical to Aunt Alice's. Molly opened the door, shouting, "I'm home!" Her father was sleeping in a big chair in the corner of the living room, a newspaper in his hand. A tall, thin man with a long, sad face. He didn't stir.

"Pater," Molly shouted in his ear. "This is my new friend Caroline."

He moaned a little but didn't open his eyes.

Molly laughed. "The old bugger drinks too much."

Molly's mother, a tiny animated woman, was in the kitchen, drinking a cup of coffee and smoking a cigerette. "My aren't you the pretty one," she said to Caroline, then turned to Molly. "Did you introduce her to your father?"

"Of course."

They began to laugh, as if his drinking was a joke, not something to be ashamed of, or angry, or sad about.

"Come on," Molly said to Caroline. "I want to show you something." She led the way upstairs into the bathroom and instructed Caroline to sit down on the toilet seat. "Now lean back." She put a soft black line around Caroline's eyes, some mascara on her lashes, a little powder on her cheeks, a touch of rouge, and finally, some very red lipstick. "There, you could pass for eighteen."

Caroline looked in the mirror, pleased. "I'll show you something," she said, grabbing the powder puff from Molly's hand. She dabbed a little on her lips, then applied a second coat of lipstick. "There, that way it will last for hours."

Molly sat down on one of the twin beds that took up most of the floorspace in her room and pulled a package of cigarettes from her pocket. "Want one?"

"Well...."

"I'll show you how." Molly lit a cigarette, inhaled deeply, then handed it to Caroline. "You'd better lie on your back. You'll feel dizzy at first."

Caroline did as she was told, drawing the smoke into her lungs again and again. She felt as if she was floating up to the ceiling. Her mind floating, her body still on the bed.

"I have to go to mass in the morning," Molly said.

"Can I come?"

"I don't see why not."

Molly told Caroline when to stand, when to kneel, when to cross herself. Caroline marvelled at the richness and mystery of the Catholic Church after the meanness of the United Church basement. The statues, the music, the candles and incense. The priests, the Latin, the crowds of grown-up worshippers. She felt she'd found something she'd been looking for all her life. She would become a Catholic, a nun, a Bride of Christ. She pictured herself with her head shaved. She pictured herself in a black habit, kneeling at the altar to receive communion, while her parents looked on. Her mother weeping.

"Come to CYO with me on Wednesday?" Molly whispered. "No one will know you're not Catholic. I'll say you're from out of town."

The dance was held in the hall next to the church. Young people stood around the edge of the floor, waiting for the music to start. A priest sat on a platform at the front of the hall, surveying the dancers like a lifeguard at a swimming pool watching for any sign of trouble.

"Hey, there's Louie," Molly said.

A group had gathered around a dark-haired boy, dressed in a

white shirt and black serge pants. He stood with his back to Caroline.

"Who's Louie?" asked Caroline, hurrying alongside Molly.

"Louie's going in the seminary tomorrow. He's going to be a priest. Hey Louie!"

Louie turned to them. The most handsome boy Caroline had ever seen, with dark eyes and curly hair falling across his forehead. "Hello Molly," he smiled. White dazzling teeth. A sleepy Jean-Pierre Aumont smile. His shirt was open at the neck.

"This is my new friend Caroline."

He nodded to Caroline, then turned back to the others. One of the boys slapped him on the back. "So how does it feel?" As if Louie were going off to war. Louie shrugged.

Somebody else said, "You can always change your mind and leave town, you know," and they all laughed.

Just then the lights dimmed and the music started. Couples paired off and moved away. A boy asked Molly to dance. "Louie, talk to Caroline till I come back."

One of the boys elbowed Louie. "Hey Louie, this is your last night of freedom."

Louie turned to Caroline and grinned. "Would you like to dance?"

At first he held her loosely, talking about this being his last time here, her first. Then he moved closer, until his chin rested on the side of her forehead. Then closer, until her chin rested in the curve of his neck. His body was lean and muscular, not too tall, not too short; they fit perfectly from the shoulder to the knee. When Caroline closed her eyes it was as if their bodies formed one dark warm pool of pleasure through which they glided to the strains of Glen Miller, Tommy Dorsey, Duke Ellington.

When the music stopped Caroline waited for Louie to lead her back to Molly. But he didn't move, didn't let go of her hand. They stood side by side, not speaking, not looking at each other, until the music began again. Then they resumed their journey.

Ray Eberley, Frank Sinatra, the Ink Spots. *I don't want to set the world on fire, I just want to start a flame in your heart....*

They danced all night, only dimly aware that the others were talking about them, ignoring occasional shouts of "Hey Louie!" They didn't talk, there was no need, they knew everything there was to know: he was leaving the next morning, she would never see him again, he would never hold another girl in his arms, ever. This evening would have to last a lifetime.

Nearly forty years later, Caroline and Molly sit in a fashionable cafe in Trastevere, sharing a carafe of white wine. Molly, who's been to Rome before, is making a list of the museums, galleries and historic sites she thinks Caroline should see. It's hot, more like summer than spring.

Molly pauses, her attention drawn by the young people laughing at the next table. "I can't believe how different everything is. Twenty years ago this square would have been deserted. Except maybe for an old woman in black, feeding the cats."

"The what?"

"The stray cats."

"That's what I thought you said." Caroline laughs, feeling a bit lightheaded from the wine. The pain of her divorce is like part of another life. "Let's share another carafe of wine."

"No," Molly says. "I want you to see the Vatican Collection and the Sistine Chapel."

They cross St. Peter's Square, past groups of black-clad priests, into the coolness of the the cathedral. They pause inside the door while their eyes adjust to the sudden gloom.

"When were you last in church?" Caroline asks.

"I can't remember. Years. You?"

"My father's funeral."

A young priest genuflects before a side altar. Caroline watches as he walks toward the front of the cathedral, his cassock tight across his back and shoulders.

"Do you remember Louie?"

"The one who entered the seminary?"

Caroline nods. "You know sometimes I think Louis was the

love of my life."

Molly laughs. "You're joking."

"No, I mean it, I really do. No false hopes, no disappointments, no fears. Just three hours of perfect bliss."

The Burial Plot

The cemetery is one of the oldest in the city. Tall elms and maples shade turn-of-the-century tombstones. Benches are placed at intervals along winding pathways overgrown with spirea and lilac. The whole enclosed by a wrought-iron fence. Quite beautiful really, Liz thinks grudgingly.

Brian clutches the pamphlet he showed her at breakfast. *Prearrange your own funeral, it says. Spare your loved ones needless anguish and expense; people in the throes of grief do not make wise consumer choices.*

"It makes a lot of sense," he says. "What if we were suddenly killed in a car crash?"

Liz doesn't answer. They've had this conversation before. She's told him what she thinks: it's morbid. She also thinks it's busywork, something to fill his time, although she hasn't told him that.

"We have insurance. You didn't object to that."

"Brian, let's just get it over with. I don't want to be late."

"Of course not." With mock concern.

Liz ignores this. "Where's the sales office?"

The sales office is located in an ivy-covered Victorian gatehouse. Mr. Emery, the man in charge, tells Brian the plots in the lower price bracket are down the hill in the new section. Brian asks to see one. "We won't need anything fancy."

The new section is like a suburb—treeless, recently sodded,

its limits defined by a link fence. On the other side cars zoom along a six-lane expressway. People on their way to work, Liz thinks. Brian chooses a small plot. "We'll be cremated," he tells Mr. Emery. "All we need is space for a marker."

Liz pictures their names inscribed on a square of granite sunk into the ground. This *is* morbid, she thinks. And annoying. Ever since she went back to school, it's been one thing after another. First the renovations, then the landscaping, now this.

Brian had announced his plans 'to put their house in order' two weeks after her classes started. The children needed a place to play on rainy days, he said, he needed an office at home. Sam and Katy could have used a place to play on rainy days when they were eight and ten, not at twelve and fourteen. And Brian needed an office less than he ever did; business was slow, nobody was building, nobody was hiring architects. Liz had suggested they save the money for a rainy day, knowing he wouldn't listen. Once Brian made a decision about something, he did it no matter what—as if to change his mind were to admit defeat.

He had spent the next few weeks drawing up plans, calling Liz at school almost every day to ask her opinion about colours, fabrics. The art school she had chosen was small and informal, telephone calls were allowed, but Liz found the frequent interruptions embarrassing and disruptive. She'd be in the middle of a drawing or the beginning of a painting and get called to the office. She asked Brian not to do this unless it was an emergency. "This concerns you too," Brian said irritably, as if by being at school, away from home, she was shirking her responsibilities. Brian had encouraged her to go back to school. "Go for it, you're good. You really are. And it's something you've always wanted to do." But he'd been busy then.

A crew of workmen arrived late in November, the worst possible time for Liz: end of term projects had been asssigned, Christmas was coming up. She consoled herself that it would keep Brian occupied. And it did. He supervised the workmen, made them coffee, talked to them about the sorry state of the industry. When they moved out in February, they wished him all the best. "Enjoy your family room," they called to Liz. The family room was in the attic, Brian's office in the basement, complete with kitchenette, bathroom, and outside entrance.

"I'm going to enjoy working here," Brian told Liz. He was shortlisted for a municipal pavilion, the sort of building he did so well, and they were both confident he'd get it. But the project fell through—the client opted for a more conservative look.

The following week Liz arrived home from school to find a second crew of workmen breaking up the sidewalk. "What's going on?" Brian informed her quietly that he had decided to replace the concrete with flagstone and have the wooden fence that bordered their front replaced by a wrought-iron one. "That way it won't have to be touched for another twenty years." All it needs, Liz thought hopelessly, is a coat of paint.

He had also drawn up plans to landscape the entrance to his office, he told her. "Brian, where is the money coming from?" He looked at her coldly. "If worst comes to worst, I suppose we could use some of yours."

He doesn't mean it, Liz thought.

She had worked as an interior designer before she met and married Brian. Since then she'd done the odd bit of work for him, for free of course. Recently her old boss had hired her on a freelance basis. Nothing very demanding, but the pay was good. She had managed to put aside enough money to pay for her tuition and supplies for the next two years.

Liz and Brian walked home from the cemetery in silence. Once inside, Brian poured himself a cup of coffee, leaned against the kitchen counter and looked around. "My life doesn't have any meaning."

Nothing more to do on the house, Liz thought.

Brian looked at her, his eyes beseeching.

Oh God, he means I don't give his life meaning. What next? "Another person can't give you that, Brian."

"But love can."

Or work, she wanted to say. Once he gets a new contract, he'll be fine. He loves me and the children when he's working.

She glanced at her watch; she was not going to miss another day of school, they would have to talk about this later, after the children were in bed. She hurried to the hall closet and exchanged the dark coat she had worn to the cemetery for an old sweater of Brian's. A bulky off-white Irish knit, which she pulled on over her peach T-shirt and burgundy cords. The sweater was huge on her, but the colours pleased her. She pulled her hair free and tucked it behind her ears, thinking maybe it was time to have it cut.

"What are you going to do about this mess?" Brian called from the kitchen. The counter was stacked with dishes; the dishwasher, they both knew, needed emptying.

Why the hell don't you do it, she wanted to say, but a voice inside her cautioned, Take it easy, he's having a hard time. He's not like this when he's working. She pictured Brian on the way out the door for a meeting with a client, dressed in his new suit, exuding a sense of importance. "Give me a hug," he'd smile. When had she last heard that?

"I'll clean it up when I get home." She gathered up her portfolio and the tubes of watercolour she had bought the day before.

The moment she stepped out the door she felt better. The simple act of walking along the street, running to catch the streetcar, filled her with pleasure, a sense of being alive, part of the world that for so many years had been filtered through Brian and the children. Not that she regretted it; she had wanted to stay home with the kids. In fact, she had wanted one last baby, but Brian had convinced her the time for babies was past. Now of course it was. She would be forty-four on her next birthday.

The school was everything Liz had hoped for. A wonderfully informal, big open space, where she drew for hours on enormous sheets of paper or in small sketch books. Satisfying a need she had overlooked for years. Most of the models were young, energetic dancers, all line and movement. But the model that morning was an enormous black woman, completely at home in her body, unapologetic about her weight, not trying to please anyone but herself. Beautiful, Liz thought. The teacher stopped to look at her drawings. "Look at that line," he said. "You're a natural, why have you waited so long?"

Liz shrugged, smiling. Why? Her parents, solidly middle class, affluent citizens, had insisted she study interior design rather than painting. That way she could always get a job and do a little painting on weekends. Which somehow she never did.

"Terri, look at this," the teacher said.

Most of the students were in their early twenties. Terri was twenty-six or seven. A skinny little thing dressed in black leather like a biker's girl, her hair pulled back in a ponytail. Liz liked her. Liked her crazy black and white drawings. They had lunch together occasionally, Terri had come to her home once or twice. "So, you're an art student by day, a middle class matron by night!" Liz had laughed and begun to apologize. "Don't apologize. I think it's great."

Terri studied Liz's latest work. "It's great," she said. "I don't know about the colour though."

Liz had splashed a little watercolour on the drawing. "You know I'm afraid of colour," she said.

"If it's that important to you," the teacher said, "you're probably a colourist."

A colourist? "Do you think so?"

"I do. It's what you should concentrate on next year."

Next year. An image of Brian sitting at home waiting for the phone to ring popped into her head. How long was this going to last?

The last week of school Brian announced that he was going up to the cottage for a few days. Alone.

"Brian, our wedding anniversary is on Saturday."

"I'm very tired," he said firmly. A small contract had come through; he'd been working night and day, although rarely in his new office. "I'll come down on Friday for you and the kids."

"Well, I suppose you deserve a rest." She rather liked the idea of being on her own for a few days. She would invite Terri, the teacher, a few other students to dinner, to celebrate the end of term.

But Terri didn't show up at the studio that week.

Brian was very quiet on the way up to the cottage. His eyes seemed to glaze over whenever Liz mentioned school. She thought it was probably a good thing classes were over for a while.

After dinner Brian built a fire and entertained Sam and Katy with stories about the summer jobs he'd had when he was a student. The summer he worked in a logging camp, the summer he organized a strike, the summer he came face to face with a grizzly bear. But when they laughed and asked for more, Brian shook his head and glanced mournfully at Liz.

"I'll go up and make the beds," she said, shaken; she had never seen him look so sad.

Their bed had been stripped. Now why would Brian do that? The sheets were hardly used. Besides, making the beds was her job. Brian had always been very fussy about the division of labour.

She went to bed before Brian. He wanted to read a bit, he said, he'd come up later. She woke in the middle of the night with a sense of alarm. Brian was beside her but they weren't touching anywhere. They were turned away from each other, hugging the outside edges of the bed. Usually, no matter how things stood between them, they slept wrapped round one another, spoonstyle, their need to be close stronger than anger, more constant than sex.

The next morning Brian drove into town by himself, he'd forgotten something he said. Hours later he called to say he'd run out of gas. He'd done it before, leaving her to entertain the children in the car while he went in search of help. "I'll go ahead with lunch," Liz laughed. It was late afternoon when his car drifted along the driveway. Liz watched from the living room window. She turned as he entered. "What took you so long?"

"You'd better sit down." Brian said. "I've got some bad news I'm afraid."

"What is it?"

"I've fallen in love."

We will do this with dignity, Liz thought, like two adults, and sat down like someone in a trance.

"With Terri."

Terri? Her Terri? It wasn't possible.

"She's coming up on Monday to spend some time with me here." He paused to light a cigarette.

"Brian, we've got to talk about this."

"I've made up my mind. As soon as I can manage it I'm going to take a small apartment in town so we can be together. Sam and Katy will stay with you in the house of course."

"She's in and I'm out. Just like that?"

"I'm sorry."

Sorry! Liz got to her feet. "I want to go home."

"I'll drive you down tomorrow."

"No. I want to go now."

Liz sat huddled up against the car window, sunglasses in place, while Brian explained to the children that Mother had to go back to town. Neither Katy nor Sam said a word; Liz could tell they knew something was up.

"I'll bring them down tomorrow when you're feeling better," Brian said, putting the key in the ignition.

On his way to pick up Terri, the voice inside her said. She couldn't believe that Terri was a real threat. Little Terri, with her boyish body and those Orphan Annie eyes. Those terrible clothes. "Terri mustn't feel guilty. She's not to blame," she blurted, out of some crazy loyalty to their friendship. The significance of the sheets hadn't struck her yet. It wasn't until she was safely inside the house, and Brian had started back to the cottage, that it hit her. She looked at her watch. It would take him an hour to get there. She opened a bottle of wine and sat down to wait. When the hour was up, the bottle was three-quarters empty. Brian answered the phone immediately.

"Terri was up at the cottage with you."

"Yes."

"You were fucking that chick in the family cottage." Chick. Where had that word come from?

"We'll talk about this later."

"We'll talk about it now! If you wanted a dirty weekend, why didn't you go to Buffalo?" She felt as if she'd been peed on by the two of them. "You really are a couple of sleazes."

Brian hung up.

She dialed again. He didn't answer.

Why has she done this to me? Liz raged. I opened my home to her, encouraged her with her drawing, told her things. She remembered the day she introduced them. Brian had come in just as Terri was leaving.

"Stay and have a drink," she said to Terri.

"I don't drink," Terri answered in a no-two-ways-about-it tone of voice.

"A cup of tea?"

"A glass of water would suit me just fine." Terri sat down curling her legs beneath her.

"What'll you have?" Liz asked Brian. "The usual?"

Brian smiled at Terri. "A glass of water will be fine for me too."

"A glass of water?"

"A glass of water."

Liz went in search of two glasses of water for them, a glass of white wine for herself. When she returned, Brian was expounding his latest theory about authority. "Authority and role are inseparable. You can't have one without the other. The authority invested in any role, whether political, social, artistic...."

Liz had heard this before. Many times before. "I don't agree at all," she said impatiently. "As far as I'm concerned, authority comes from skill or talent."

Brian reached for his glass of water, annoyed.

"I don't think women worry about authority," Liz continued recklessly. "They don't work that way. They just dig in and do whatever needs to be done." Liz had worked with other women when Sam and Katy were in nursery school, a co-op nursery. "They co-operate."

Brian bridled. Terri smiled mysteriously.

"Anyway, that's been my experience," Liz concluded limply. "What about you Terri?"

Terri put her glass on the table. "I've gotta go."

"Can I give you a lift?" Brian asked.

"No thanks. I've got my bike."

Brian watched from the window as Terri unlocked her bike and rode off down the street. "Well, what do you think?" he asked, turning to face Liz.

"What do you mean?"

"What's she like? Is she talented?"

But that's not what he meant, she thought now. That's not *all* he meant. She poured herself another glass of wine, went upstairs to their bedroom, and opened the closet door. One by one she took his suits and jackets, ties and shoes, and threw them down the stairs. When the closet was empty, she phoned her neighbour Caroline. Caroline's husband had been gone for over two years. "Mum's out of town," one of the kids told her. She called Jo-Anne further down the block; no answer. As a last resort, she dialed Judith's number. Judith's divorce had just become final.

"Brian's left me," she wailed into the phone. Judith said she'd come immediately.

"He's abused you," Judith fumed, opening another bottle of wine.

"No, Brian never did that."

"He has abused you, emotionally."

To make her point, Judith told Liz about the night she found her husband "fucking a perfect stranger" on a couch outside their hotel room. "I screamed, 'What are you doing?' He looked right at me and said, 'What does it look like I'm doing?'"

"He actually said that?"

Judith nodded primly. "We'd gone to a lodge in Muskoka to try to patch things up." She sipped her wine. "What is it about men?"

I've called the wrong person, Liz thought, reaching for the bottle. This isn't helping.

She woke the next morning with a terrible headache, and the realization that she would have to lug Brian's clothes back upstairs before Sam and Katy arrived home. Only then did it occur to her that their wedding anniversary had come and gone.

Brian came the following weekend to collect the kids; he looked pale and haunted—a tortured, angry man. Liz's heart lurched. Her mother, who had come to stay, watched from the window. "Brian looks awful," she said, her voice shocked, reproachful. "Old and tired."

Minutes later a friend telephoned to say Brian had dropped by to return a book. The friend didn't know about Terri. "Brian looks terrific," she said. "Ten years younger. I asked him what he'd been up to."

There was a knock at the door. It was Brian's best friend David. David's car was parked in front of the house, his wife Sandra waved from there. They've been up at the cottage, Liz thought numbly.

"I've instructions to deliver this," David said, his tone a cross between his usual jaunty charm and an apology. He handed her a small bag containing an assortment of things she had left at the cottage—an old bathing suit, a toothbrush, face cream, a robe and nightgown.

"Are you okay?" David asked.

"I'm fine. Really."

The moment she closed the door, she howled. David and Sandra have been staying at the cottage with Brian and Terri.

The thought of Terri in her bed of seventeen summers drove her wild. All day long Terri's face seemed to hover in the air around her. And at night Liz dreamed about her. That she had hired Terri to help her paint a mural, something about a ship and dead birds; they were working in the little house Liz and Brian had rented when they were first in love. Terri stood by the fireplace waiting for instructions. Liz noticed the smell of menstrual blood.

"You have your period," she said. (Her own were becoming irregular.)

"Yes." Terri smiled smugly.

She shouldn't be here, Liz thought. "I won't be needing you anymore." She pulled out her chequebook. "How much do I owe you?" Terri walked toward her, her smile lewd, her eyes white and glassy. Thyroid eyes, Liz thought, noticing how much weight Terri had gained, that she was now quite plump.

"If this is to be my last day," Terri said, "Don't you think we should have a friendly drink?"

Liz shot out her foot and kicked her away. "You were at the family cottage, you were sleeping in my bed."

"Yes," Terri replied, pleased with herself.

"Get out of my house."

Terri sat down, tucking her feet beneath her. "Do you mind if I stay a little longer? Someone's picking me up."

"Get out!" Liz screamed and shoved Terri out the front door. But when she turned around, Terri was coming in the back door. She threw her out again, Terri came back in again.

"What if Katy sees you behaving like this?" Terri taunted.

"Get out!"

Smiling, Terri sat down outside and waited. The little house suddenly transformed into the cottage. Brian came striding along the driveway, looking very slim and dapper.

"Give me a hug," he said to Terri.

"I can hear every word you're saying!" Liz shouted through the keyhole.

Katy refused to go out of the house once she knew about Terri. She refused to answer the telephone when her friends called. "Do you know how embarrassing this is?" All day long she sat in front of the television watching soap operas. Abandoned wives confiding their anger and grief to anyone who would listen. Husbands falling into the arms of younger, prettier women. When Liz finally decided enough was enough and disconnected the television set, Katy just sat there, staring at the empty screen.

Finally she said, "This place is a mess! I'm going to vacuum."

And she did, first the living room, then the dining room. Katy, who usually had to be persuaded to pick her clothes up off the floor. Maybe she thinks that's why Brian left us, thought Liz. Maybe it was. She studied photographs she'd taken of Brian before he told her about Terri, looking for clues.

Two weeks later, Brian phoned to say he wanted Sam and Katy to spend the weekend at the cottage with him and Terri. Liz told him Sam had been invited to spend the weekend with a schoolfriend and she thought it was too soon for Katy. "Nonsense," he said. "I'll pick her up tomorrow at five."

"What if I don't like her?" Katy panicked.

"You don't have to like her, Katy," Liz said, quoting a handbook Caroline had lent her on how to help your children deal with separation and divorce. "It won't change the way your father feels about you. He will always love you. *You* haven't done anything wrong, you mustn't think that. Anyway, I'm sure you'll like her, Katy. She's young, lots of fun. And she'll like you." She'd better like you, she thought grimly.

"This is the second worst day of my life," Katy wailed.

Liz was curious in spite of herself. "What was the worst?"

"The day Joe died." Joe, the family dog, had died at the cottage the summer Katy turned eleven.

Liz resolved to tidy up while Katy was at the cottage. Brian had suggested she rent his new office; she went downstairs to see what needed to be done. There were boxes of clothes the children had outgrown, discarded toys, Christmas decorations. Cross country skis Brian had bought for the whole family, a dollhouse he had started to build for Katy. Architectural drawings Liz had done for him. It was worse than reading old love letters.

Katy arrived home looking quite cheerful. "Terri's not ugly," she said.

"What? Who said she was?" Liz said.

"She's nice," Katy said.

"Please, don't talk to me about Terri."

Katy stared in disbelief.

"Do you talk to Terri about me?" Liz asked, trying to sound reasonable.

"Of course not."

"Then why talk to me about her?"

Katy's eyes filled with tears. "You said you wanted me to like her." She turned to run out of the room, Liz reached out to stop her.

"Oh Katy, I'm sorry. I *do* want you to like her. It's just ... these things take time. It's going to be all right."

Katy pushed her hand away. Liz lit a cigarette, something she hadn't done in front of Katy for a long time.

"You're smoking," Katy said. "*Everything* is different."

"Katy, I'm going through a difficult time."

"So it's okay to smoke. You didn't mean what you said. I guess I'll smoke when I grow up."

Liz put out her cigarette.

Katy was very quiet. "I can't talk to my dad anymore."

"Katy, I'm sure you can."

Katy shook her head. "He's always with her. She doesn't suit my dad, she's too young for him. I don't understand why he likes her."

"I think we need a little holiday together," Liz said quietly. "Sam goes to camp next week. I'll find us a nice place where we can lie about the beach all day, swim, read. We'll have a lovely time. Just the two of us." Liz and Katy had never been on a holiday without Brian and Sam, the suggestion felt unreal.

Caroline recommended a lodge at the tip of the Bruce Peninsula. It stood at the edge of a village, a collection of small, unimposing buildings huddled together along the waterfront. The lodge itself was a cross between a motel and a summer camp. A busload of elderly travellers had just arrived. A young couple in white shorts and matching T-shirts headed for the tennis courts. A greater contrast to the seclusion of the cottage Liz couldn't imagine.

The desk clerk assigned Liz and Katy the lower half of a "chalet," a Swiss-style cottage furnished with colonial maple furniture, worn shag carpeting, orange drapes and throws, all a bit the worse for wear. Stale cigarette smoke hung in the air; overhead a small child toddled back and forth. Liz was dismayed but Katy loved it on sight. She settled in like a child playing house, deciding she would sleep on the pullout couch, Liz could have the bedroom. She opened and closed the kitchen cupboards, checking to see if anything had been left behind. Liz told her she could buy whatever she wanted for snacks in the village, they would eat meals in the dining room.

Dinner that night consisted of frozen vegetables, French fries, deep-fried chicken balls, pie and ice-cream. Katy loved that too. Afterward, they sat on their own little veranda playing cards, watching the man from upstairs fly a kite for his small son. A couple, arms around each other, walked along the the waterfront. A huge steamer appeared on the horizon.

It's alive, it's cheerful, it's unpredictable, Liz thought. It *is* going to be all right, I'm going to be all right. It's not so bad to be without a man. I can come and go as I please.

"Let's come every year," Katy said, resting her head on Liz's shoulder.

"Why not," Liz smiled.

But back at home her thoughts were bitter. "My husband's left me for a younger woman," she told friends, neighbours, the woman in the corner store. If they believed it, perhaps she could too. Close friends like Caroline, Jo-Anne and Judith heard the story of the sheets. Her resentment was growing like a tumour.

She set up a still life in the new family room in the attic and tried to paint, but all she could think was, My marriage has fallen apart, what am I doing up here? What made me think I wanted to do this? Painting's not that important to me. I don't even know I have any real talent.

One Sunday a few weeks later Brian phoned to say he was running a bit late, but he would try to have Sam and Katy home in time for dinner. At a quarter to six, his car pulled up in front of the house. Sam and Katy were in the back seat, Terri in the front next to Brian. Her hair, now blond, hung loose to her shoulders, backlit by the afternoon sun; she was wearing a printed top. Liz stepped out onto the porch.

Smiling, Brian got out of the car and sauntered casually toward the trunk. Sam came up the walk toward her. "Hi, Mum," he said sheepishly and hugged her. Brian followed, carrying Katy's bag. Liz opened her mouth like someone possessed, like a ventroliquist's doll, and out came: "Don't you ever bring that bitch here again!" Loud enough for the whole street to hear.

Sam pounded the wall with his fist. Katy turned and ran across the street into the park. Liz stepped back into the house, shaking. You've got to stop this, she told herself, you've got to pull yourself together. Stop acting as if you're the first woman ever to be left by her husband. This is the eighties. Marriages don't last forever anymore. Not even second marriages.

Over the next few weeks she bought herself a pile of the new self-help books appearing in her local bookstore. *How to Forgive Your Ex-Husband and Get On With Your Life, How To Be Your Own Best Friend, The Challenge of Being Single, Why Do I Feel Like Nothing Without a Man.* And as long as she was reading, she felt okay. The books made it so easy to see where she'd gone wrong, giving up her own life, expecting Brian to make her happy. She must learn to love herself, that's where happiness lay.

But one morning, when she'd finished one book and hadn't found another, she woke up with tears streaming down her cheeks and only the vaguest memory of a long, shadowy dream in which she was stranded, trying to get home. This has all been a dream, she thought. Brian is going to walk back in the door and we'll carry on our life together, as it should have been, not as it was.

I miss him, I want him to come home. The nice, loving, modest, funny man I married, not the cold, judgmental man in that photograph.

Get out of bed, her strong self countered. Go to the 'Y,' get some exercise, go for a swim.

I'm afraid.

I'll look after you.

I can't live alone, I really can't.

Of course you can. Anybody can. If Brian were still at home, you'd be lying awake wondering how much longer you could put up with him.

I want him to love me, that's all I ever wanted. Without him, I don't know who I am.

You're acting like a little girl, abandoned by her father. A relationship has ended, that's all.

Not a relationship, a family. I want him back.

When? In the morning, reading the newspaper while you make breakfast?

No.

At night then, talking about his work while you make dinner?

Well, no...

What you miss is a nice warm body in bed, that's all. Now stop this stream of consciousness shit. Get out of bed this minute.

Liz pictured Sam and Katy on their way to the cottage with Brian and Terri. I want to go with them! I'll sit in the back seat with Sam and Katy. Terri can have my place, I don't care. Katy and Sam and I will go for long walks, gather wildflowers, make pancakes and bacon to surprise them....

The telephone rang. "This is Mr. Emery."

"Who?"

"Mr. Emery from the cemetery. I hope I'm not disturbing you. I would have called sooner, but I've been away on holidays. I'm afraid there's been a bit of a mix-up in my absence."

"A mix-up?"

"A man's wife was buried in the plot I sold you."

I'm dreaming, Liz thought.

"A terrible mistake, I can't imagine how it happened. I haven't notified him yet. I was hoping you'd consider exchanging it for another. That would save us the trouble of digging up the woman's ashes and spare her husband a trip from Sudbury to bury her a second time. Of course if you don't want to do that...."

No, I don't want to. The burial plot was Brian's idea, he can deal with it. Then she pictured the man in Sudbury. Probably some poor old guy, who had really loved his wife. Who'd been loyal to her through thick and thin. And now he was all alone.

The plot Mr. Emery offered her was in the new section, farther down the hill, closer to the highway. Ugly.

"You really don't have anything else?" she shouted over the noise of the traffic.

"Well, as a matter of fact, we've just opened some space up above. Perhaps you might prefer one of those."

They walked back up the hill. Small plots now lined a path in the old part of the cemetery near the gatehouse. Liz chose one shaded by a tall maple, close to a lilac bush.

"It's lovely, Mr. Emery. It really is. But something has occurred to me..."

"What's that?" he asked warily.

"The names on the deed will have to be changed."

"Changed?"

"Yes, changed. Changed to Brian Lord and ..." And what? Brian and Terri? "To Brian Lord and friend." Laughter bubbles up inside her. "And sent to Mr. Lord at his new address."

"His new address?"

"I'll give it to you."

"And another thing. I think Mr. Lord would prefer the plot you showed me in the newer section."

"You do?"

"I do."

She turns away to hide her smile, and for the first time notices what a beautiful morning it is. A lovely fall morning, light and clear. Light clouds moving quickly across a clear sky. A cerulean blue sky, the trees dark green with patches of cadmium orange. In the park across the way, a black and white dog is chasing its tail. A child tossing a ball in the air—his windbreaker a single spot of crimson in an expanse of emerald green.

I am a colourist, Liz thinks joyfully. I really am.

One Form or Another

Dr. Copeland's office is on the ninth floor of a tall glass building on a busy downtown corner. Suite 909, a standard one-bedroom apartment being used as an office. There's a four-piece bathroom inside the door and the space occupied by the receptionist's desk was obviously intended for a bed. Jo-Anne finds this strangely disquieting.

Mrs. Davis, the receptionist, is a woman in her sixties. White hair, sensible blouse and skirt, no attempt to appear younger. Jo-Anne wonders why Dr. Copeland hired someone her age. To save money? Or because Mrs. Davis is well past the problems that torment most of his patients.

"Dr. Copeland will be with you shortly," Mrs. Davis smiles. "Why don't you take a seat."

There's a pile of dog-eared copies of *Time* and *MacLean's* on the coffee table. Jo-Anne checks the dates. Some are two years old. She begins to wonder if Dr. Copeland is the right choice. If she should have come at all. She's been looking for salvation in one form or another all her life. Maybe it's time she gave it up.

She thinks of the prayer meeting her mother held in their house the year she turned five. She can still remember standing in the living room in the midst of tall, dark, looming strangers and looking up at the preacher—a gaunt pale thin-lipped man, dressed in black. "Jesus came into the world to save sinners," he told them.

Whatever happened to the poster he gave me, she wonders. A picture of Jesus—a smiling bearded man in white and blue robes, with long dark curly hair—surrounded by little children. Beneath the picture the words, "Suffer little children to come unto Me."

Those children are sinners too, she'd thought then.

A few days earlier her mother had caught her with both hands under the cover, comforting herself the only way she knew how. Her mother warned her she'd be punished if she ever did it again. And although Jo-Anne had wondered how her mother would ever know, she knew instinctively that her guilty pleasure—that place down there that had no name, that her mother never touched when she bathed her—was what sin was all about.

She wanted to be saved.

She almost was the summer her family moved to Keewatin Street, next door to Doreen Mather, across the street from Penny Nichol, whose house backed on Sherwood Park. She was nine years old. One afternoon Penny invited her and Doreen to watch what she did with her thirteen-year-old cousin in the park. Her boy cousin. Tall and lean in long trousers, the legs of a man attached to the torso of a child.

He strode ahead, like the Pied Piper, down wooden steps, past family picnic tables, over a bridge and along a path into the woods. He stopped when they reached a small, dappled clearing. "Don't look till I tell you," Penny told Jo-Anne and Doreen. They turned their backs and waited. Jo-Anne wished she'd stayed home, playing monopoly or looking after her baby sister. She heard Penny's cousin ask, "Where are you?"

You? The word burned between her legs.

"Okay. You can look now."

Penny's back was arched against a small embankment. Her cousin stood between her legs, the front of his trousers loosened, bending over her.

For a moment nobody moved, nobody said a word. Then together Jo-Anne and Doreen turned and ran, as if the schoolbell had rung, or as if they'd seen a ghost.

A few days later Doreen invited Jo-Anne to a crusade. "What's a crusade?" she asked. "It's to fight the devil and save sinners." That sounded wonderful. "I'll have to ask my mother first."

Her mother said she could go if she promised to behave herself. Jo-Anne said she would. "Well then, go and put your dress on." Meaning Jo-Anne's good dress. Powder-blue muslin, trimmed with lace. Her best shoes were black patent leather and her ankle socks were white. Her mother combed her hair into pigtails, tying each one with a white ribbon, then pressed a dime in her hand for collection.

The crusade was in the People's Church, a big stone Gothic building on Bloor Street where the Manufacturer's Life Insurance building now stands. Jo-Anne and Doreen sat side by side up in the balcony, leaning forward to watch people stream up to the altar to be saved. Young people, people as old as Jo-Anne's mother and father, some even older. Jo-Anne was shocked. What sins could they have committed?

"You must die to the temptations of this world," the minister thundered.

She thought of Penny and her cousin.

"You must be born again in Jesus." The minister raised his eyes toward the balcony.

He's looking at me, Jo-Anne thought.

"You must seize the moment, it will not come again."

The choir began to sing. *Softly and tenderly Jesus is calling, Calling for you and for me; Patiently Jesus is waiting and watching ... Calling, O sinner, Come home.*

Jo-Anne stood up. "I'm going down," she whispered to Doreen. God would take away the itch between her legs. She would never play with Penny Nichol again, she would never go near Sherwood Park again. "Excuse me, Mrs. Mather," she said to Doreen's mother.

Mrs. Mather grabbed her by the arm. "Where are you going?"

"I'm going down. I'm going to be saved."

"Oh no you don't." Mrs. Mather pulled her back to the seat. "You'll have to ask your mother first."

The door to Dr. Copeland's office opens. A businessman, his face averted, hurries to the hall closet for his coat. Dr. Copeland smiles encouragingly at Jo-Anne. He's a tall man in a grey suit, his complexion sallow, his hair receding.

He looks tired, thinks Jo-Anne.

"I'll see you in a moment," he says and slips into the bathroom.

Jo-Anne notices a door opposite the bathroom, which is closed. She wonders if it's a kitchen, if Dr. Copeland keeps food in there for lunches. From where she is standing, she can see into his office. He's furnished it with old Swedish modern, the kind of furniture she and Dan had bought for their apartment. Dr. Hussain's office was furnished with antiques.

It's almost twenty years since she first saw Dr. Hussain, afraid that the new therapeutic process, the new panacea to which many of her friends were turning, wouldn't work for her. But it did; she enjoyed lying on the couch, sorting out her feelings, talking about her inhibitions. She had tried two psychiatrists before settling on Dr. Hussain. One, an aggressively handsome man of fifty, wanted to know if her grandfather had ever molested her. Her dear gentle grandfather. The other, an elderly man, talked endlessly of penis envy. Dr. Hussain said almost nothing. No talk of sexual abuse, no talk of penis envy. No talk of sin, Dr. Hussein was not Christian. An essential qualification. Jo-Anne blamed most of her problems on the Christian church. Her mother's church.

Nothing she told Dr. Hussain shocked him. In fact, he laughed out loud at her most shameful memories and advised her to go home, take a mirror and examine "that place down there." Within a year of her first appointment she was married to Dan, doing everything she could to become pregnant. That's where happiness lay. Happiness and the only kind of immortality, she had concluded, humans could hope for.

Together she and Dan tracked her fertile days, then made love on the big bed he'd made them from a slab of six-inch rubber foam, a sheet of plywood, and four concrete blocks. Afterward she'd lie on her back, buttocks raised on a pillow, knees to her chest, in a desperate attempt to prevent Dan's seed from escaping.

Month after disappointing month.

"Sorry to keep you waiting," Dr. Copeland ushers her into his office, motioning her into the chair in front of his desk. The fabric on the arms of the chair is threadbare, the carpet shabby. Is he hard up, she wonders, or just plain stingy. Maybe he doesn't care. Is that good or bad?

"Well, what seems to be the problem?"

Jo-Anne delivers the speech she has prepared for this moment. "Nothing pressing. I've a wonderful husband, two wonderful children. I just feel I need some meaning in my life over and above family and friends, house and garden. To express myself in some direct, personal way."

Should she tell him about the dreams she's been having lately?

Dreams in which she discovers parts of the house she hadn't known existed. A stairway to a suite of rooms, open, airy, waiting to be claimed. A doorway to an adjoining house, dark and dingy from neglect. The hallway cavernous. Empty. Scary. The night before she'd dreamt about the stairway again. That she had moved her desk to the top landing and started typing. A novel, it seemed, her own.

"I've always wanted to write but...."

"But?"

"I don't know. I guess that's the problem."

She'll be forty-three in less than two weeks. It's now or never. The children are both in school all day. She helps out in Richard's bookstore the days he lectures at the university, but he could hire someone else to do that.

"What's stopping you?" Dr. Copeland probes.

She shrugs. "Somehow I just don't feel I have the right."

"What do you mean, right?"

"I can't explain."

He smiles. "Why don't you try."

"It's as if I don't have the same rights as other people. I feel somehow … cut off from the rest of the human race. I really can't explain."

"Well, we'll talk about this later." He scribbles something in a notebook. "How long have you been married?"

"Fouteen years." Jo-Anne relaxes, glad to be dealing in facts. He writes that down. "How many children do you have?"

"Two. A boy and a girl. Mark and Amy. They're adopted."

That interests him. "Tell me about that."

"Mark was six weeks old when we adopted him. A beautiful baby. I loved him from the moment I laid eyes on him." He was everything she wanted. He would fulfill her longing for a child, reconnect her to the human race, end the shame of her infertility.

"And did he?"

"Yes and no. It helped that he looked like me. Everybody said so." Everybody except Richard's mother, who took endless photographs of Mark the weekend they flew to see her. Then pulled out family albums to show her photographs of Richard as a child, photographs of Richard's uncles and aunts and cousins. *This is the musical one. This is the one who had polio. This is the one who became a lawyer.* Jo-Anne imagined her showing photographs of Mark to future visitors. *This is the adopted one.*

"What about Amy?"

"Amy's very pretty, very bright. Long and thin with red hair and brown eyes. She doesn't look like me. Not at all." She forces a smile. "I found it harder to forget that she was not my child, that she had a mother of her own out there somewhere." In the beginning scarcely a day had passed when she didn't think about Amy's mother.

"And Mark's mother?"

"No, I thought about Mark's father. But that was different. I felt sure he would like me, that we would like one another."

The thought of Amy's mother had filled her with a sense of failure. A sense of being judged. She shrugs. "Of course I hardly ever think about their parents now they're both in school and I'm working in Richard's bookstore."

Dr. Copeland is not interested in Richard's bookstore. "Why did you decide to adopt?"

"Why does anyone adopt?"

"Are you infertile, or is it your husband?"

"Oh no, it's not Richard. I mean, Richard is my second husband."

"Tell me about your first husband."

Jo-Anne shrugs. "His name was Dan Wentworth. A nice man. I met him when I was working at the university bookstore. He was a postgraduate student, came in often. We talked, he asked me out for coffee, we discovered we both liked Buñuel films. The usual story." She shrugs again. "We were both lonely. Both shy. He wanted to be a geologist. I wanted to be married, have a baby."

Dr. Copeland is writing quickly. He pauses and looks intently at her. "What went wrong?"

Jo-Anne looks away. "Everything. Fertility tests, a miscarriage, an ectopic pregnancy." She sighs, picking away at a thread on the arm of her chair. "It went undiagnosed for almost five months."

Dr. Copeland is startled. "An ectopic pregnany? Are you sure?"

"Yes. I guess it wasn't such a common occurrence then. My doctor thought it was just a tricky pregnancy, that I was overly anxious. He advised me to stay in bed, try not to think so much. Dan was away, studying rocks. I stayed in bed with my two cats. One morning the pain was unbearable...." She takes a deep breath. "I knew something terribly wrong had happened. I'd hemmorhaged although I didn't know it then. Somehow the rupture sealed itself off."

"You're lucky to be alive."

Jo-Anne nods. The doctor who operated, the one Dan took her to see when he came home, said almost the same thing. But when he added there would be no more babies, she wasn't sure she wanted to be. It was as if all the fears she'd confided to Dr. Hussain had come true. She was defective, a failed woman. Nothing good would ever come out of her. That sweet presence inside her had been a grotesque mistake.

Even now, she could hardly bear to think of it.

"Dan was very kind," she says finally. "He cleared everything away while I was in the hospital—the baby clothes, an old cradle we'd found in the country, a teddy bear I'd bought." There is a pause, then, "When I came home, it was almost as if it had never happened."

The sound of Mrs. Davis typing fills the silence.

Dr. Copeland waits for her to continue.

"But we never made love again. When Dan was offered a job at the University of Manitoba, I moved into an apartment of my own. They gave me my old job back at the bookstore. I met Richard there about a year later."

He had come into the store to order some textbooks for his English class. They had known each other only three weeks when he proposed. She had been careful to hide her flaw from all but her closest friends, her closest women friends, but she couldn't do that to Richard. She said there was something he should know. He smiled as if there was nothing she could say that would make a difference.

"I told him I couldn't have children."

"How did he take it?"

"His exact words? That changes things." She shrugs again. "Of course it did, what kind of man would willingly marry an infertile women."

"Not all men want children."

"This was the sixties, Dr. Copeland. Two-career, childless couples were not in vogue. If you didn't have a husband, a baby in your arms, you were nothing."

Dr. Copeland lets this pass. "Well, how did you respond?"

"To Richard? I told him, That's the way I am, take it or leave it." She had stood up and crossed the room so Richard wouldn't see how she was feeling.

He was right behind her, saying, "I want you just the way you are. I won't pretend it doesn't matter, of course it matters. But we can adopt." Jo-Anne thought she would have died if he'd said anything else.

Dr. Copeland looks at his watch. "Would you like to talk about your ectopic pregnancy?"

"No, I don't think so."

"It might be a good idea." His voice is gentle.

"I'm sorry, I just can't." She has started to cry.

Dr. Copeland hands her a kleenex and waits. "When did this happen?"

"Seventeen years ago."

"You're talking as if it was yesterday."

Dr. Copeland suggests another appointment.

Jo-Anne hurries to the bathroom, splashes cold water on her face, and looks at herself in the mirror.

The day the pregnancy test came back positive, she'd stripped before the bathroom mirror, hers and Dan's, to study her breasts for any change in her nipples, any new fullness. She had turned sideways, thrusting her belly out as far as it would go. This was what she'd always wanted, this was what she was meant for.

Jo-Anne takes the elevator down to the lobby then pushes through the revolving doors to the street, squinting against the bright sunshine that bounces off the windows of passing cars. As she steps onto the sidewalk she could swear a voice calls out to her. "Lest Ye be born again, ye shall not enter the Kingdom of Heaven."

A voice from her mother's prayer meeting.

"Birth is often used as a metaphor for personal salvation," Dr. Copeland says. "Your confusion is understandable. Perhaps that explains your sense of … your sense of not having the same rights as other people."

Could it really be as simple as that? Jo-Anne can't bear it. The thought that her mind has tricked her. The thought that the church has been in control all along. Her mother's church. She had joined the Anglican Church as a university student in an act of defiance. And in the beginning she enjoyed it, exulting in the rituals, the mystery of the communion service, the restrained elegance of chapel. But not for long. Whatever the liturgical differences, she soon concluded, the message was the same: Jesus came into the world to save sinners, so repent. She hasn't been near a church in over twenty years.

Dr. Copeland says, "You must have talked to someone about your ectopic pregnancy."

Jo-Anne shakes her head. You've lost one of your functions, the surgeon told her. She knew she'd lost much more than that. Adopt, her friends told her. A child is a child, there's no difference. There was a difference, she knew, a big difference.

"How did you feel?" Dr. Copeland asks.

"I felt as if I was carrying my baby—stillborn—inside me."

"And now?"

"The same."

Dr. Copeland hands her a kleenex. "Was it a boy or a girl?"

"I don't know. I didn't ask and they didn't tell me."

Dr. Copeland shakes his head. "It's a loss our society is only beginning to acknowledge." He pauses, waiting for her to say something more.

There was nothing more to say.

"A lot of my patients are dealing with death," Dr. Copeland says. "People with unresolved mourning. Quite often the death of a child, for which none of us are prepared." He pauses. "Some of my patients have formed a support group for grieving parents. Perhaps you would care to join them. Yours is an unusual case but I'm sure...."

"No."

He raises his eyebrows.

"No."

"Well." He tries again. "One couple I see have donated money to a fund in memory of their child. That seems to have helped."

Jo-Anne shakes her head. "No, what I'd really like to do is bury my baby and that's not possible."

Dr. Copeland watches her. "I'm not so sure."

On her way home Jo-Anne stops by the cemetery. The office, her neighbour Liz has mentioned, is in the Victorian gatehouse near the chapel. Inside a pale young man is sitting behind a large desk, copying figures into a ledger. He looks as if he should be selling shoes, she thinks.

"I want to buy a plot."

The young man hollers toward the rear of the room. "Mr. Emery!"

A stout middle-aged man in a brown suit hurries from the back. He looks as if he should be selling tickets in a smalltown railway station. It doesn't matter, she tells herself. It doesn't matter.

"I want to buy a plot," she repeats. "How much will it cost?"

"That depends," Mr. Emery answers. "What sort of urn do you have in mind?"

"I don't need an urn."

"I'm sorry. Regulations require...."

"It's for a sort of memorial," she says quickly. "I want to put a marker on it. Something very simple." Her eyes are beginning to burn.

Mr. Emery shows her different kinds of stone and styles of engraving and tells her how much each will cost. She chooses pink granite and the simplest form of lettering. He hands her an application form.

"What would you like engraved on the marker?"

She prints, *Baby Edwards-Wentworth, November 21, 1964.*

"1964?" Mr. Emery is startled. His assistant looks up from his ledger, his glance shifting from Jo-Anne to Mr. Emery then back to Jo-Anne.

"1964," she repeats.

A truck stops in front of the chapel and two laughing Portuguese workmen begin to unload some two-by-fours. Jo-Anne turns to watch, glad of the diversion.

"Well, that seems to be in order, Miss Edwards." Mr. Emery seems embarrassed. "The marker shouldn't take more than three weeks." He gives her a copy of the sales order, consults a map, then asks his assistant to show her plot number 71F. It's down the hill, he explains, in the new section.

The assistant leads the way, rambling on to Jo-Anne about how much he likes his job, helping people deal with grief. She does her best to ignore him.

Plot 71F is one of a row of freshly sodded treeless plots, adorned with a scattering of plastic flowers. "Don't you have anything up the hill?"

"Fraid not. We're all sold out."

Sighing, Jo-Anne says, "This is fine."

"Good. Mr. Emery will call you when the marker is in place."

That night, after the children are in bed, Jo-Anne tells Richard what she has done. "I know it's a bizarre thing to do, but Dr. Copeland thought it might help and I..."

He looks at her as if she were a stranger. "I don't know what to say. I had no idea...."

After her initial confession of infertility, they never discussed it again—there didn't seem to be much point. Nor had they ever talked about the children they might have had—a little girl with Jo-Anne's blond hair, a dark rangy boy like Richard. Jo-Anne had kept her sorrow to herself. The fault, after all, was hers.

"I just thought you should know, Richard."

The afternoon Mr. Emery called, Richard offered to drive her to the florist's to buy some flowers. She chose a bouquet of pink roses and baby's breath. They drove to the cemetery in silence.

"Shall I come in with you?" Richard asks.

"Do you want to?"

"Of course I do."

She has no difficulty finding the marker. There it is, a square of pink granite set in the ground. Richard kneels and places the flowers on it, then stands awkwardly to one side, like a distant relative.

The little grave looks unbearably sad.

Jo-Anne takes a deep breath.

Richard reaches out and takes her hand. "Let it go, Jo-Anne," he says, putting put his arm around her. "Let it go."

Jo-Anne leans against him, closes her eyes, and mourns her babies. All her babies, not just the one whose heart beat for a little while inside her.

Smiling, Jo-Anne tells Amy, "You can wear your new party dress." It's Easter Sunday and they're going to church. Something Amy has wanted to do for some time, but—with Richard's approval—Jo-Anne has resolutely refused to allow it. She didn't want her children growing up with the terrible sense of sin she had as a child. She decided early on to just stand by and watch them grow as nature intended—happy, free, without guilt.

Richard, rather surprised by the turn of events, has nonetheless offered to drive them to St. James Cathedral. He and Mark, who has no interest in going to church, will have a bite at the market and pick them up later.

They arrive at the church minutes before the service is to begin. A large Victorian building standing on a square of grass, an oasis of green in the grey and dusty heart of the city. The only people in sight are hurrying toward the church. The entrance to the church is crowded. Mostly middle-aged and elderly couples. "I guess we should have come earlier," Jo-Anne says apologetically.

Just then an usher approaches, offering Amy and Jo-Anne a seat up near the front of the cathedral. Jo-Anne takes Amy's hand and they follow him to a pew near the altar, where three elderly women make room for them, smiling in welcome.

The altar is banked with Easter lilies, the air alive with music. Joyful, measured, holy music. Amy presses against Jo-Anne in excitement. A procession, led by the bishop, carries the Paschal candle up and down the aisles of the cathedral to drive away the gloom of Lent. Their robes are magnificent. White and gold, black and scarlet. Clouds of incense explode toward the ceiling.

Jo-Anne is awed by the beauty, the sense of history. People the world over are gathered to celebrate this moment, she thinks, as people have done for almost two thousand years. Why have I stayed away so long?

"In the name of the Father, the Son and the Holy Spirit." The bishop, an imposing man with a crown of thick grey hair, rises to deliver his sermon.

Here it comes, Jo-Anne thinks, anticipating a diatribe against sin.

The Bishop asks them to think back to that first Easter long ago. To think of the disciples, running toward the tomb—think of the sound, the sound of footsteps on hard packed earth—only to find the stone had been rolled away, the tomb empty. He asks them to imagine what the disciples must have felt as they gazed at that empty tomb. "A sign that Jesus had triumphed over death, over humiliation and suffering. A symbol of hope for all of us." The bishop pauses. "How many of you have a stone in your heart?" he asks quietly, compassionately. "How many of you would like to roll that stone away, to open your hearts once more to life and hope?"

Not a word about sin.

"Let us pray."

Jo-Anne kneels, noticing the old woman next to Amy who has remained seated and is leaning forward, eyes closed, smiling peacefully. Behind her, sunlight is filtered through stained glass. Brilliant reds and blues, greens and yellow depicting scenes from the life of Jesus. Jesus healing the sick, Jesus with little children, Jesus raising the dead, defying the elders of the temple. In the window above the altar, He presides over the Last Supper. Above the Last Supper, separated by a bold arc of translucent turquoise, Jesus ascends through white clouds toward a golden palace, accompanied by a choir of angels.

Amy nudges Jo-Anne. "Where are they going?"

People have begun to file up to the altar. Jo-Anne points to the window above the altar and whispers the story of the Last Supper to Amy. How the night before He died, Jesus called his disciples together, took bread, broke it, and gave it to them, saying, 'This is my body, which is given for you. Eat this in remembrance of me.' "That's what they're going to do now," she says. "In memory of Jesus. It's called communion."

"Can I go?" Amy says.

"You can't," Jo-Anne says quickly. "You have to have special lessons first. It's called confirmation."

Several girls walk by their pew. One looks no older than Amy.

"They're going," Amy says.

Perhaps the rules have changed. If sin is no longer in fashion, perhaps confirmation is no longer mandatory.

"Mum, can I?" Amy begs.

Jo-Anne glances around the cathedral. The music is quieter now. Gentle, reflective music. She thinks of the Crusade, Mrs. Mather grabbing her arm, refusing to let her be saved. Well, I'm the mother here. "Amy, did you understand what I told you about the Last Supper?"

"Yes," Amy says quickly.

Too quickly. "Well…. Okay, follow me."

Jo-Anne leads the way to the altar. They kneel side by side at the communion rail and Jo-Anne shows Amy how to hold her hands to receive the host. One hand across the other, palms up, close to her heart.

Jo-Anne's turn comes first. She repeats the short prayer she'd been taught years earlier, asking forgiveness for all her sins, promising never to sin again. With head bowed, she places the wafer in her mouth, surrendering to the holy powers that grip her.

She senses a slight pause, a certain stillness, and lookes up—past an expanse of white and gold brocade to a small wizened face looking down at her from under a high conical hat. A mean face. He nods toward Amy.

"Has she been confirmed?"

Jo-Anne glances at Amy who waits with eyes downcast. Surely he wouldn't turn her away, at the altar, in front of the whole cathedral? That would be worse, far worse, than being scolded by Mrs. Mather up in the balcony.

Amy looks up to see what's causing the delay.

Jo-Anne wishes they'd never come. She wishes they were at home eating Easter eggs, or walking in the park. She takes a deep breath, looks the minister in the eye, and lies. "Yes."

It's clear he doesn't believe her, but what can he do? Stop communion and argue? Demand proof? What proof?

After what seems an eternity he places a wafer on Amy's hand and moves on to the next kneeling figure. Jo-Anne watches Amy raise her hand toward her mouth.

"Is this right?" Amy whispers, loud enough for everyone at the altar to hear.

Oh God.

The minister turns and glares at Jo-Anne. The sin be on your head, his eyes seem to say.

I have sinned, Jo-Anne thinks. I've told a barefaced lie on the altar of God, seconds after receiving holy communion, after vowing never to sin again. How could I? What was I thinking? Amy shouldn't be here, she hasn't been confirmed. Remorsefully, she looks at Amy.

Amy is smiling, as radiant as a bride.

Jo-Anne wants to hug her then and there. What does it matter if she hasn't been confirmed? Jesus wouldn't mind, I'm sure he wouldn't mind.

Landmark Days

Liz finds it in a pile of junk mail on the hall table, sandwiched between a flier for anti-wrinkle cream and a warning about termites. One of the kids must have put it there. An envelope, hand delivered, from Elizabeth Stoddart, Barrister and Solicitor. Inside a six-page, double-spaced legal document stating that Brian's petition for divorce has been heard and granted, the terms of their separation will continue to be binding, both are free to remarry one month from the date of the hearing. Which, she notices, took place place on January the 6th. It is now January the twenty-eighth.

She's been divorced for three weeks without knowing it.

What was I doing on the morning of January the 6th? she wonders. Sixteen years of her life had been undone, surely she felt something. She checks the calendar. The 6th was a Friday. She must have been at work, sitting at her desk or drinking coffee in the cafeteria. Possibly on her way to the bank to deposit her paycheque. Indecent, she thinks.

No, indecent isn't the word. Perhaps there isn't a word for what she's feeling. It's like the day she heard her Uncle Stan had died while she was out of town—he'd been dead and buried six weeks. No one had thought to let her know, no one had expected her to be so upset. She hadn't expected to be so upset. It wasn't just that Uncle Stan had died, he'd taken his memories with him, his memories of her. No one else had known her in quite the same way.

She looks again at the date on the document, calculating quickly that Brian will be free to marry Terri in nine days. He's been living with her for over a year. Almost two years.

She picks up the phone and dials her neighbour Caroline, the person she turns to more and more in moments like this.

"Jo-Anne's here," Caroline says. "We'll be right over."

Within minutes they are standing in the front hall, stamping snow from their boots. Caroline in her jogging suit, grey and baggy, Jo-Anne in jeans and a black turtleneck sweater. Saturday morning clothes.

"I know exactly how you feel," Caroline says.

"You can't know how I feel. I don't know how I feel."

"You're going to be fine. Just fine. I'll throw a party to celebrate."

"Celebrate?"

"Not your divorce, silly. The beginning of your new life."

"I would never have thought of it that way," says Jo-Anne, grateful that Richard is still with her. Caroline has been on her own for almost four years. It shames Liz to think how little she helped Caroline when Tom left. Caroline said she didn't want to talk about it and Liz chose to believe her. Nobody wanted to identify with her pain, to think it could touch them. Divorce, the threat of divorce, had begun to seem like a virus sweeping through the neighbourhood.

"I'll put the kettle on," Caroline says. "What do you want, coffee or tea? "

"Whatever you like." Liz sinks down on the chesterfield, thinking how lucky she is to have friends at a time like this.

Jo-Anne stands watching her. Blonde beautiful Jo-Anne, as resolutely slender and fit as Caroline is unapologetically plump and comfortable. "I *can't* imagine what you're feeling," she says finally.

"That's okay. There's no reason why you should."

In the kitchen Caroline thinks about the day she discovered Brian had left Liz. How awful she felt. Worse, in a way, than when Tom left. That was the end of her marriage; this might be the end of the neighbourhood.

"Call whenever you need help," Brian had told her the day Tom took his stuff from the house. "We're right next door."

She'd been careful not to do that too often, but it had been comforting to know she could, the thought of Brian and Liz living happily next door oddly reassuring: it wasn't marriage per se that had gone wrong, just hers and Tom's.

Then, less than two years later, Brian too was gone. Run off with a perfect stranger. She'd been out of town, so it wasn't until her taxi pulled onto the block that she knew. There was Liz putting out the garbage. "Hey, Brian should be doing that," she called.

Liz looked stricken. "Brian's gone."

"Gone where?"

"He's left me." She checked her watch. "I've got an appointment. I'll call you when I'm back. I'm so glad to see you."

The taxi-driver helped Caroline carry her bags into the house.

Her briefcase was overflowing with notes. A month's work. A month of travelling around, talking to women in their forties and fifties about their hopes, their fears, their new found strength, as well as their new vulnerability. "I've never felt better in my life," one woman had told her. "All the role playing over. I feel as if I got myself back." Another said, "You're really on your own. Gender has turned against you. Men are no longer your allies."

Caroline had refused to believe this.

Brian wasn't just her neighbour, he was her friend. In the last few years she'd been closer to him than to Liz in a way. The day before her trip began, he'd come to the door to wish her luck, in his hand a copy of *Conundrum*, the account of Jan Morris's mid-life sex change. "Something to read on the plane," he grinned. On the cover was a black and white photograph of Morris, smiling, arms crossed under her new breasts, a purse over her shoulder, her posture confident, happy, strong.

Caroline shook her head. "Why would anyone choose to become a middle-aged woman?"

Brian glanced at the ladder leaning against the wall; Caroline had been changing a lightbulb, a last minute chore. "I must say I admire the way you're managing on your own."

"I couldn't have managed without you and Liz."

Brian looked away.

That was the last time she'd seen him. Brian the good neighbour. Brian the devoted husband, the loving father. The kind of father she'd wished for as a child. The kind of husband Tom never was.

The kettle boils. Caroline fills the teapot, stacks three cups on a tray and walks back into the livingroom where Liz and Jo-Anne are sitting side by side. "We'll celebrate the day the decree becomes absolute," she tells Liz. "It's one of those landmark days."

"That's what you said about Christmas."

"Did I?"

"You did. We were at Jo-Anne's, remember?"

Jo-Anne was kneeling in front of the fireplace, trying to get a fire going. Caroline and Liz were sitting on the sofa. Richard had gone off to a meeting, so they felt free to talk.

"It's one of those landmark days," Caroline told Liz. "Like the day you divide up the furniture. Or the day you sign the separation agreement. The day your divorce comes through. Talk to any divorced woman and she'll tell you the story of her first Christmas alone."

"I'm dreading mine," Liz said.

"You'll be all right. But it's important to be prepared, it really is."

Jo-Anne stood up. "There. That should burn for an hour or two. I'll be back in a minute. I promised Amy I'd tuck her in."

Caroline and Liz watched her hurry upstairs. "Our conversation is making her uncomfortable," said Liz.

Caroline shrugged. "What have you planned for Christmas day?"

"I'm spending it with my mother, my children, and Jennie."

"Jennie? That's nice." Brian's daughter from his first marriage. She'd flown over from London to spend Christmases with Brian and Liz for as long as Caroline had known them.

"Jennie wrote to say she'd stay with me as usual, if it was all right with me. All right? I'm delighted."

"Good."

"The children will spend Christmas Day with me, Boxing Day with Brian and Terri."

"That sounds sensible," Caroline said. "Just make sure you buy yourself something for under the tree. You don't need Brian to buy you gifts, you know."

Liz bought herself an expensive art book and a bottle of Vent Vert by Balmain. She bought the children what she knew they wanted, plus a few little surprises. A black T-shirt for Sam, a tape of old Bob Dylan favourites for Katy, who was in love with the sixties—she couldn't believe Liz had lived through them and not gone to Woodstock. She bought silver earrings and a silk batik scarf for Jennie, a sweater for her mother. Then she phoned her mother to discuss Christmas dinner.

"I'd like to cook a goose for a change but I'm not sure the kids would like it."

"Christmas is not the time for changes," her mother said firmly. "Would you like me to stuff the turkey?"

Brian always did that Christmas morning, dressed in his blue and white striped chef's apron, the radio tuned to their favourite FM station, filling the house with Christmas music.

"I'll make the kind I always make, sage and onion," her mother said. "If that's all right."

Brian made chestnut and sausage stuffing.

"Sounds wonderful."

"Have you got your tree?"

The tree. How was she going to manage the tree? Always on Christmas Eve Brian and Sam would drive to the corner and buy the biggest tree on the lot. Which was invariably too big; when they got it home Brian would have to trim a foot or two from the bottom. "You can use the branches to decorate the windows," he'd say, as if he'd planned it that way. Next he'd fill an old tin pail with coal and, while Katy and Jennie watched, he and Sam would manoevre the tree into the pail.

"Is it straight?" he'd ask Liz.

"Not quite. A little to the right. I mean, the left."

"Which?"

"The left."

Proud to be of service, Sam would hold the tree in place while Brian looped a rope around its trunk and fastened it to the doorframe. Exacting work. Men's work. It took about an hour.

"There, how's that?" Brian would ask.

Invariably Jennie would say, "I think it's the nicest tree we've ever had," and they would all agree. Pleased, Brian would pour himself a brandy and sit down to watch while the girls helped Liz decorate the tree. Women's work.

Well, now she and the children would have to do both.

A week before Christmas, Liz asked Sam to go to the corner with her to get the tree. She didn't want to wait till the last moment. She slipped a measuring tape into her purse so she wouldn't have to trim any from the bottom.

"You can choose," she told Sam on the way.

Sam chose a Spruce and together they dragged it home, its branches trailing in the snow. Inside Sam held it upright while Liz went down to the basement to get the pail.

That was when she noticed the stand. Heavy iron in the shape of a cross with a small container in the centre. A Christmas tree stand. Where had that come from? Then she remembered: it had been attached to a tree Brian bought late one Christmas Eve, so late it was the only tree left on the lot. Why did we never use it again? Liz wondered, carrying the stand upstairs.

Jennie and Katy, who had been sorting Christmas decorations into handy piles—tinsel balls, angels, coloured birds, miniature toys, lights—paused to help Sam lift the tree onto the stand. He gripped it firmly while Liz tightened three large screws designed to hold it in place. It stood upright in less than five minutes.

They all laughed in amazement.

"I don't believe it!" said Jennie.

"What was that all about? All that stuff with the coal and the ropes and the…" said Sam.

Katy shrugged. "Don't ask me."

They turned and looked at Liz as if she'd know. "It's probably the way his father did it," she said. "It's the way my father did it."

Christmas morning, Jennie was delighted with her earrings, Liz's mother with her sweater, and Sam with his T-shirt. But nothing seemed to please Katy. Not even the Bob Dylan tape.

"You can change it for something else if you like," Liz suggested.

Katy shook her head. "It's not that." She glanced toward the window. "This just isn't my favourite Christmas. Not enough snow, I guess."

Liz looked at Jennie, who had once told her that when she was Katy's age she used to wish her mother, Helen, and Brian would get back together for Christmas. That was the present she wanted. One of the nicest Christmases Liz can remember was the year Jennie attached a letter to her gift, telling Liz and Brian she'd come to accept their marriage and her place in it.

Well, now Jennie would have to accept another marriage, the confusion of three families.

Sam pulled his new black T-shirt over his pyjamas. His dark hair curled down over his shoulders; on his upper lip the beginning of a black moustache. He reminded Liz of a photograph of her father as a young man. Katy and Jennie took after Brian's family.

Sam smiled. "Your present isn't under the tree. I'll bring it down," he said, running upstairs to his room.

"Do you know what it is?" her mother asked Katy.

"Uh, huh," said Katy with a smile.

Sam brought down a rubber plant, the sturdy variety, bred to withstand just about anything. He'd tied a big red ribbon around it.

"Sam, it's lovely!"

"It will bloom in the spring," he told Liz proudly.

She gave him a hug. "That's very thoughtful of you. Thank you."

"I thought you'd like it."

He watched, pleased, as she put it in the window to catch the light. "I bought two Birds of Paradise for Dad and Terri," he said innocently. "If it's all right, I'll change and take them over now."

Liz pictured two long stemmed birdlike blossoms—the most beautiful, the most exotic, the most erotic of all flowers. Birds of Paradise for them, a rubber plant for me. "No, it's not all right!" she heard herself saying.

"Why not?"

"Because you're supposed to spend Christmas day with me, Boxing day with your father. You can take the flowers to them tomorrow."

"Liz...," her mother cautioned.

"But Mum," Sam pleaded. "They won't be as nice tomorrow."

"Then you should have bought them something more sensible." She turned away. "Like a rubber plant."

Jennie began to gather up her presents. "I'll make some tea," she said quietly.

"Mum," said Katy, "You're being mean."

Mean and ridiculous, Liz thought miserably.

"Liz, let the boy go."

"All right," said Liz, pretending to make a decision. "You can go if you promise to be back by three."

Sam's face flooded with relief. "Thanks Mum."

He dashed upstairs and came back a few minutes later in jeans and a sweater, carrying the flowers. He rested them on the hall table, quickly pulled on his boots, grabbed his coat, picked up the flowers again and hurried out into the snow.

Liz watched him go, aware that the others were watching her. For one awful moment she thought she was going to cry.

On Christmas morning, in front of Katy and Jennie. In front of her mother.

"I'll be down in a minute," she said.

Her bedroom was one of the few dependable comforts in her life at the moment. For months after Brian left, she'd gone on sleeping in their room, their bed, their sheets. A warm burgundy colour, warm but not feminine. Suitable for a master bedroom, for the master's bedroom. Nothing irreversible had happened, that room seemed to say, Brian could walk back in anytime. Until one night she couldn't stand it any longer. She dismantled the bed and dragged it across the hall to the spare room.

"Mum, what is it?" Katy called from her room, half asleep.

"What's going on?" Sam demanded, sounding just like Brian.

"Go back to bed," she told them, angling the bed to face the park.

The next day she searched the stores for new sheets. *Her* sheets. White and frilly with eyelet trim. That night she lay in bed thinking, Brian's never slept in these sheets, in this room. The window was like a magic box, the tree beneath the streetlamp glowed a wonderful golden-orange. Intimations of happiness and peace, she thought then.

Well now the trees were bare, the ground hard and dry beneath the snow. What would Caroline say? You can buy yourself two Birds of Paradise. You can buy yourself a dozen Birds of Paradise. You don't need Brian to do that. Besides, by the time your rubber plant blooms in the spring, their Birds of Paradise will be just a memory.

Lurking beneath the surface of her mind was the hope that Terri was just a phase, that once Brian found his way through the door to middle-age he would come home.

That was the present she wanted.

Five months later Brian phoned to tell her he'd started divorce proceedings. "I want that settled," he said. "I've hired a lawyer, a woman. Her name is Elizabeth Stoddart. She'll be sending the petition for your signature. Let her know if you find any mistakes."

"I'll look at it when I have a moment," Liz said, as if she had more important things on her mind.

As soon as the envelope arrived, she tore it open. The petition was written on a standard form, like a lease or a mortgage. She scanned it quickly. In the space intended for her date of birth, Brian had written Helen's date of birth. He'd written Helen's family name instead of hers.

She dialed Brian's number, her hand trembling. "You lived with me for sixteen years," she said angrily. "Surely you can remember my name!"

"I'll have my lawyer look after it," he said coolly and hung up.

Liz phoned Caroline.

"I felt like a ... like an old-age pensioner complaining to the bank manager about a mistake on my welfare cheque."

"That's how he wants you to feel," Caroline said. She reached over and filled Liz's glass. "Or maybe he really is confused. Maybe he's in a bad way. There's a word for it. The something of confusion...."

Jo-Anne put her hand over the top of her glass. "I won't have any more."

The three women were sitting around Caroline's kitchen table, the doors open to the garden. A beautiful day in May, the air still, fragrant.

Liz could tell they were making Jo-Anne uncomfortable again. She remembered how, when Brian was still with her, she'd felt threatened whenever Caroline talked about Tom leaving.

"Crisis of confusion," Caroline blurted. "That's it."

"I never have any trouble remembering names, dates, that sort of thing," said Liz. "Muscle memory."

"Muscle memory? What in heaven's name is that?"

"Well, that's what the self-help books call it. When I got depressed, I thought, what happened in May? What didn't happen in May. Brian and I got married in May, Brian left me in

May. Brian told me about Terri in May." She sipped her wine. "That's muscle memory."

"I'd call that reflex memory," said Caroline. "The body remembers."

Jo-Anne looked from Caroline to Liz.

"All the time I was with Brian," said Liz. "I used to count the years we were together against the years he'd spent with Helen. They were married for sixteen years."

"I didn't know that."

"They were together for sixteen years, they were married longer. Anyway, after Brian and I had been together for three years, I figured Helen still had thirteen years seniority on me, after ten, it was down to six, and so on."

Caroline hooted with laughter.

"Finally, the weekend of our sixteenth anniversary, or the sixteenth anniversary of the year he left Helen, whichever way you want to look at it, I thought, We're even. Helen and I are even! That was when he left me for Terri."

"That says something about *his* muscle memory," Caroline said drily.

Liz opened her mouth to say something more, something funny, but closed her eyes. Caroline leaned over and put her arms around her.

Jo-Anne studied her empty glass.

Liz wiped her eyes on her sleeve then grinned at Caroline. "I sometimes wonder about Terri. Maybe she's counting, maybe not. I do know that when their sixteenth anniversary rolls around, Terri will be forty-four and Brian will be seventy-one."

Caroline grinned back. "I wouldn't count if I were her."

"I think you're both terribly brave," said Jo-Anne. "I don't know how you manage, either of you."

Caroline settled back in her chair. "It gets easier as time goes by. As a matter of fact, while Liz was talking it occurred to me that I'm no longer recovering from my divorce. It's something that happened in my past. Tom is part of my history—like my father or my brothers."

"Congratulations," said Liz.

"Well, it's taken almost four years."

"Richard would never leave me," Jo-Anne said. "Marriage is too important to him. The family, children. It's everything to him."

"I would have said the same about Brian," said Liz.

A moment of silence, then Caroline spoke up. "In some ways, Liz, the second year is harder, in some ways easier. You'll no longer wake up thinking about Brian every day—it'll be every second day. And the questions you ask yourself will change. Will he come back one day or will I miss him for the rest of my life? becomes have I lost the only man in the world for me or am I well rid of him?"

"Which is it?"

"I'm well rid of Tom."

"Is that really how you feel?" asked Jo-Anne.

"Most of the time."

"But you loved him. You thought he was the right man for you."

"I knew marriage and a family were right for me. I wasn't so sure about Tom."

Liz is amazed. "That's exactly the way I felt. Do you suppose all women our generation felt that way?"

Nine months later, on February 6th, the divorce is final. It snows. Big soft white flakes that cling to the window for an instant then melt. Caroline phones to ask Liz if she has thought of anyone else she wants to invite to the party. The new couple on the block are coming, the gay couple who used to live on the block, a man from Caroline's office—a jovial man and a wonderful storyteller—and Jo-Anne, whose husband Richard has stunned them all by leaving.

"I can't think of anyone," Liz says. "What can I bring?"

"Nothing silly. You're the guest of honour."

It's a lovely party. Caroline has poached a salmon, Jo-Anne has brought dessert, everybody has brought champagne. The conversation is warm and optimistic, with lots of laughter. Talk about the children, work, movies, a trip to Mexico the new couple plan for February, a trip to Italy the gay couple made the previous fall. No mention of Brian. Or Richard. The only reference to divorce is when the new couple joke that probably the only reason they're still together is that they're just too old and tired to start again.

This could have been a terrible evening, Liz thinks, standing at the door, preparing to leave.

She hugs Caroline. "Thank you."

Jo-Anne is watching her.

She's watching me to see how I'm managing, to see how she'll manage, Liz thinks.

She hugs Jo-Anne. "You'll be fine," she whispers.

Un Bel Di...

"Why did you choose such successful women?"

Caroline has just screened her first film, "On Clear Ice," to an audience of women in their forties, fifties and sixties. An upbeat look at menopause—exploding many of the myths circulated by the pharmaceutical companies, it celebrates the new sense of well being among women in mid-life. Not yet well-documented. What one woman in the film called "the best time of my life." Another said she felt she was "on clear ice and could skate forever."

"I honestly didn't think of them as successful," Caroline replies. "All have problems. Most of them live alone, some below the poverty line. What makes them 'successful,' I suppose, is their optimism, their courage."

"You chose not to talk to them about the problems facing women of a certain age. Poverty, joblesness, desertion," the viewer continues, her tone almost hostile.

"That's not the film I wanted to make. We all know about the downside."

The woman who arranged the screening intervenes. "Caroline, did you find it difficult to get women to talk about menopause?"

"No. Not at all. Which surprised me. Menopause was not something we talked about in my family. Or menstruation for that matter. When I got my first period, my mother made it clear that no one, not even my brothers, was to know about it. I knew without asking that my last period was nothing to write home about."

The audience laughs.

"When it happened, I found myself feeling stronger and better than ever. Like a twelve years old kid, glad the cosmos was no longer surging through me. Almost all the women I talked to felt this way."

There's a moment of silence.

Another woman puts up her hand. "I'm just an ordinary housewife and my husband has just left me. I was terrified but now that I've seen your film I'm no longer afraid."

If I'd made the film for you alone, Caroline thinks, it would have been worth it.

She wonders suddenly how Miss Maxwell would have liked the film, if she were still alive. As always, the thought of Miss Maxwell fills her with regret. And shame.

Caroline entered Miss Maxwell's class the year she turned sixteen. 1946. The war was over. Her father had come home the previous spring, wearing a light grey, double breasted suit he'd bought to replace his navy uniform. He hadn't had a drink in three years. His body was lean, his moustache trimmed like Robert Taylor's. He looked like a movie star himself. "I'm through with selling," he told them. "I'm going to start a business of my own."

That was before Charlie White dropped by, a bottle of whisky in his back pocket. "Heard ya was home. The fellas and I are gettin' together for a little game tonight. Thought ya might like to join us."

After that the grey suit hung in a closet while her Dad played poker with Charlie and his cronies—day after day, night after night. Usually at Charlie's but occasionally at home in the dining room, a bottle of whisky on the table, the air thick with smoke.

Caroline hated Charlie White. He was a dirty, smelly, foul-mouthed man. *Goddamn this, goddamn that, ain't that sumpin,* wouldn't that rot your socks, eh? Hey missie, can you take your nose out of that book long enough to get us an ashtray?

Miss Maxwell spoke with a slight English accent. Her r's and a's glamoursly soft, her voice rising and falling in a melodic way. Her hair was cropped short and she wore a grey tailored suit—not unlike Caroline's Dad's. "I'm officially Anglican, unofficially atheist," she told them. (People in Queen's Corner where Caroline lived all went to the United Church.) She had been educated at St. Anne's College, a branch of Epiphany College, and before coming to Carlton High, had taught in a private girls' school in Toronto.

She reminded Caroline of a mystery she'd read during the summer. A mystery set in an English college, where educated men and women sipped sherry in oak-panelled libraries and spoke of literature, music and art.

Miss Maxwell stood at her desk, left hand hooked in the pocket of her jacket, and read aloud:

You promise heavens free from strife,
Pure truth and perfect change of will;
But sweet, sweet is this human life,
So sweet, I fain would breath it still;
Your chilly stars I can forgo,
This warm kind world is all I know.

"Well." She smiled brightly. "I'm here to teach you English composition and literature. Victorian literature. We shall begin with Hardy's *Tess of the d'Urbervilles*. But first I want to put that novel in perspective."

She walked to the bookcase and removed a book about ancient Greece and Babylonia, a time and place, she said, where sexuality was considered not sinful, but divine. An attribute of the gods.

A ripple of interest ran through the class.

"A time when intercourse was thought to make women holy."

Intercourse. Caroline stared at the floor, her cheeks burning.

Most of the boys in the class were farmers' sons; they knew all about intercourse—the animal kind if not the real thing. From the corner of her eye she could see Jack Boynton poking his finger through the circle he'd made of his left thumb and index finger. Smirking.

Miss Maxwell held her book in the air, as if it were a piece of evidence or a declaration of war. "This, you will find, represents the antithesis of the attitudes we will be exploring in *Tess of the d'Urbervilles*. It may challenge your views—your parents' views—on religion, women and pleasure. So be it."

At recess the corridor buzzed with rumours. Miss Maxwell had been kicked out of her last school. Miss Maxwell had inherited a lot of money. Miss Maxwell had been engaged to an army officer killed in the war. She was older than she looked, she was younger than she looked.

The next morning there was a record-player on her desk. And on the blackboard she had printed,

Music, when soft voices die,
Vibrates in the memory—
     Shelley

"We shall begin the class with a piece of music—Massenet's Meditation as interpreted by Fritz Kreisler. Of all the instruments, the violin is most like the human voice, most suited to express human longing, desire, grief, or joy." She removed the record from its sleeve, placed it on the turntable and asked them to put their heads on their desks, close their eyes and listen carefully. A few boys snorted. She waited for them to settle down, then lowered the needle. As the music began, she walked to the window, crossed her arms and stood looking out over the schoolyard.

It was music Caroline had never heard before.

When it was over, Miss Maxwell turned and faced them. "English composition is like music," she said. "Its aim not simply the mastery of syntax, but the free expression of your innermost thoughts and feelings and experiences, good or bad."

That's not what their last teacher had told them.

"Now I want you to take your notebooks from your desks and fill a page with whatever thoughts, memories, hopes or fears come into your head."

No one wanted to do that, but Caroline did attempt to put into words the way she felt listening to the music. The violin ... she searched for words ... soared and shuddered ... like a human voice ... gripped by nostalgia and regret.

"Very nice," Miss Maxwell said.

She had tacked a list of supplementary authors to the bulletin board: Georges Sand, Jane Austen, Katherine Mansfield, George Eliot, the Brontë sisters. She offered to lend Caroline *Jane Eyre* or *Wuthering Heights*.

Caroline read *Jane Eyre* all the way to and from school, in the bus that carried her from Queen's Corners to Carlton High and back again—south on the main highway, west on No.7, north again on 47, past farmers' fields, small villages, stopping occasionally to drop students by the roadside. Oblivious to everything and everyone except Jane and Rochester, whom she felt in some strange way she had always known.

Miss Maxwell suggested she read Jane Austen next. "But you mustn't let it interfere with your homework."

Homework. Caroline had never bothered much about homework, coasting on her natural abilities. Now she began to study seriously—French, German, history, science, math, but especially English—polishing and repolishing her class essays.

In no time at all she shot to the head of the class.

"I think we have a budding scholar here," Miss Maxwell announced to the class.

Caroline decided to give up her Saturday job and concentrate on schoolwork. Listen to the Saturday afternoon opera broadcast. "Money is only money," Miss Maxwell had pointed out, "while the riches of the mind can never be taken from you."

One Saturday afternoon, halfway through *La Traviata*, her father appeared in the doorway. "Turn that damn thing off!" he yelled, striding to the radio. He switched the dial to the local station, the station that played Wilf Carter, Ernest Tubb, Rosemary Clooney. Then he took a bottle from his pocket, poured some rye into a glass and drank it straight. Disgusting. How could she hope to improve herself with a father like that?

Her mother was in the kitchen. Caroline decided to question her about their family history, in the hopes of discovering more compatible relations.

"Why do you want to know all that old stuff?"

"Because I do." People said Caroline looked like her mother—same cheekbones, same eyes. She vowed she would never be plump like her mother, never wear her hair in a bun.

"Well, what exactly do you want to know?"

"Who our ancestors were, where they came from."

"Well, your grandfather came from Belleville. His family were mostly Scots and Pennsylvania Dutch. They came up from the States. The men were bankers and gentlemen farmers."

Caroline pictured elegant men dressed in riding habits overseeing the work of hired labourers. Not like the farmers who hung around the general store Saturday nights. Not like Charlie White and his cronies. "What exactly was a gentlman farmer?"

"The women in the family never went near the barn."

"You mean the men did?" She tried to hide her disappointment.

"Of course." Her mother reached for a pie plate lined with pastry and began to fill it with the apples she'd been slicing. Her cheeks were flushed from the heat of the big black stove.

"My great-grandfather on my mother's side was English. Jonathan Lyons. He was a remittance man."

"You mean I have English blood!" Caroline was thrilled.

"Uncle Jake used to say that he was part of the royal family, that his name was really Jonathan Bowes-Lyon, like the Queen."

"The Queen!"

"Oh I don't know if it's true or not. But that's what old Jake told me."

"Why did you never tell me?"

Her mother laughed. "Caroline, you're Canadian. We've been here for generations." She sprinkled the pie with brown sugar and cinnamon. "There, that's done."

"What was Jonathan's wife's name?" Caroline asked impatiently, meaning her family name.

"Sara. Sara was a Mennonite. Their sons were called Matthew, Jethro, Andrew and John. Uncle Matt—you know, the one with the white beard in that picture I showed you—he was an itinerant minister. His children are all Americans now. Jethro—Jet we called him—was a lawyer. Andy was the handsome one. Jack was the youngest, a farmer. He was Jake's father."

"Didn't she have any daughters?"

"Oh yes. Kate, Priscilla, Jane, Alice and..." She paused, frowning. "I've forgotten, isn't that terrible. Oh, Florence, of course." She laughed. "The one I'm named after."

Caroline wondered why she never called herself Florence instead of Flo, which was so ordinary. "What about Dad's family?"

Her mother's lips tightened. "Your father's father was a horse trader from Northern Ireland." She picked up the pie, turned and popped it in the oven.

"Is that all you know about him?"

"He married a French-Canadian woman, I know that."

Caroline had read about French-Canadians in history class. French would have been better, but still.

Her mother began to tidy up.

"Did she give up her Catholicism for him?" Caroline persisted.

Flo looked up. "How do you know she was Catholic?"

"She must've been. All French Canadians are Catholic." Any fool knew that.

"I suppose you're right. I never thought of that. We never saw much of them."

Caroline knew her mother disapproved of her Dad's family almost as much as she disapproved of him. "What was he like?"

"Your grandfather? He was a handsome man, but he drank. Like all the Gibson men. Of course I didn't know that when I married your father." As if he'd tricked her, as if she would never have married him had she known. "The Gibsons were all handsome men, with high, prominent foreheads. People thought that's why they were all so smart. Maybe that's why you kids are all so smart." She filled a saucer of milk for the cat.

Caroline thought about that. All six of them had done well in school, but she was the only one so far to stick at it. Her older sister Margaret and brothers Jim and Al had quit school as soon as they could. Who knew what her younger sisters would do.

"Your father got the highest marks in arithmetic ever recorded in Elgin County, did you know that? The school authorities sent him to Toronto to have the size of his head measured," her mother said.

"He should've had his head *examined*," Caroline said.

Flo laughed, Caroline knew she would. Her father was fair game. She'd understood that for as long as she could remember. They had to choose between their mother and their father, to be on one side or the other. For all kinds of reasons, it was safer to be on their mother's side. Occasionally over the years she'd crossed the line—lured into her father's car by the offer of an ice-cream cone, a funny story, a bit of singing, a long drive. But the outcome was always the same: she'd be left sitting outside the local tavern until closing time. When he came out, acting like he'd forgotten all about her, he'd hand her a dollar bill. "Here, buy yourself an ice-cream cone tomorrow."

Her mother would be waiting at home, furious. "You get up to bed young lady, and you.... I've told you never to take that child out in the car." And off they'd go. The next morning he'd ask for his dollar back and Flo would smile her I-told-you-so smile.

Her brothers didn't have to be told. They never forgot their father was the enemy, that their role was to protect Flo from him. Not that there was much they they could do. Jim, the older of the two, was crippled, their father a big man. Still, their loyalty seemed to comfort Flo. "One day we'll fix him," they promised her. "One day he'll be sorry for the way he's treated you."

Of course now they were living and working in the city but they came home on weekends.

Well, why worry about her father when there were lawyers, ministers, perhaps even royalty in the family. She crossed to the window. The trees were bare. She could see all of Queen's Corners—the garage, the general store, the church, the backs of houses. Three years, she thought. We've lived here three years, the longest we've lived anywhere. It would be just my luck if we stayed forever.

"What do you think went wrong," she asked, turning back to her mother. "Why did we sink so low?"

Miss Maxwell wrote on her Christmas report card that Caroline was university calibre. Caroline was thrilled. She had begun to dream of studying philosophy and English in a community of scholars (which she would learn was not what undergraduate life was all about). She knew she could never afford it, but still it was nice to have her calibre confirmed.

"Do you really think so?"

"There's no doubt about it."

"I know lots of students get summer jobs in Muskoka, in big hotels like Bigwin Inn or Elgin House and they they make a lot of money, but I don't think they earn enough to…. I don't even know what the fees are."

"With your marks, you could to apply to St. Anne's for a bursary," said Miss Maxwell. "I'll recommend you."

"I'd be the first in my family to go university. Well, the first in the last couple of generations," she added, thinking of her mother's Uncle Jet, the lawyer. He must have gone.

Miss Maxwell smiled. "Someone has to be first. I've suggested the school authorities give a fifty dollar prize to the year's most outstanding student. It will be announced mid-term." Her expression implied Caroline was almost certain to get it. "That would be a start."

Her parents were not pleased. "University is a waste of time for girls," her father said, pausing on his way out the door. "Unless of course you study something useful. Like dentistry or mathematics."

Mathematics was still her strongest subject, but she didn't intend to make it a way of life.

Her mother, who had studied piano as a girl, smiled dreamily. "Go to secretarial college, get a job, save up and buy yourself a piano. Take lessons. That's what I'd do If I were you."

Caroline liked music, but had bigger plans. She'd turn herself into a nice middle-class girl and leave her messy family behind.

Miss Maxwell had set up a library of long-playing classical records in the corner of the room. Caroline borrowed *Highlights from Madame Butterfly* by Puccinni, waited until the family were upstairs in bed, then played it over and over again while she studied for exams. She loved the music, loved being downstairs alone. It was as if the house belonged to her, anything was possible.

"Un bel di vedremo...." The voice on the record was high and sweet and filled with longing. She knew more or less what it meant: One fine day my true love will come. And one fine day her true love would come. A tall dark stranger with hollow cheeks and piercing eyes. An educated man. An artist of sorts, perhaps a concert pianist. She pictured herself in a large formal room, French doors open to the sea, listening devotedly while he played Chopin on a grand piano—passionately, vigorously, consumed by his own genius.

Or she pictured herself strolling along the seashore, waiting for him to return. Never wondering where he'd gone, or where he'd take her when he returned. Or even how they'd live. They'd live happily ever after, far from Queen's Corners. The future would take care of itself, that much she knew. That much Flo had told them, in so many words: you have to be unhappy at some time in your life, so better to get it over while you're young. She herself had had a wonderful childhood and look how her life had turned out. It seemed logical enough, even in a sense fair.

Caroline heard her father's car lurch to a halt outside. The squeal of his tires told her he'd been drinking. She lifted the needle from the record, glancing at the kitchen clock. One o'clock.

The door slammed behind him. "Where's your mother?"

"Asleep." She'd been in bed for hours.

"Tell her to get down here and make my supper."

Here we go, Caroline thought. She'll refuse, he'll insist, they'll start to fight, and we'll all be awake for hours.

"Dad," she said, closing her book. "I'll make your supper."

He frowned. "That's your mother's job."

"I'll do it." She rummaged in the ice-box for leftovers—meatloaf, mashed potatoes and gravy, green peas—and spooned them into a frying pan. When she figured the food was warm, she put it on a plate in front of him.

"This is delicious," he said, his eyes bloodshot, his voice slurred. "When did you learn to cook like this?"

Caroline sat down and opened her book, her contempt for him softened by something gentler.

"What's that you're reading?" Her father didn't approve of reading.

"History."

"You spend too damn much time with your nose in a book. It's not healthy for a girl your age. You should be outside getting exercise."

She knew better than to point out it was dark outside. She glanced toward the window. The moon hung low over their neighbour's barn, silhouetting the trees at the end of the yard. "It's a full moon."

"A beautiful night," he said. "A beautiful night. I love the night."

"Me too." Startled that they had this in common, that they had anything in common.

"You know, Carlie," he said, summoning all his powers of concentration. "You and I could get along, if we only got along better."

Caroline tried not to smile. This was one of the few peaceful moments she'd ever spent with her father. She cut him a piece of pie, made him a cup of tea.

"The best cup of tea I've had in ages," he said, pulling his wallet from his back pocket. He handed her a twenty dollar bill.

Caroline thanked him, even though she knew he would take it back in the morning.

The night she came home with the fifty dollar prize, he took that too.

She'd run all the way home from the school bus, giddy with pride. Bursting into the kitchen she plunked the envelope on the middle of the table, already set for supper.

Her mother was standing at the stove. "What's that?"

"I won the prize."

Her mother wiped her hands on her apron and stared at the envelope. Caroline's name was printed in large gold letters on the outside; inside were five ten dollar bills. A lot of money in 1948.

"Caroline, put that away," she said nervously.

"The girl most likely to succeed ... a budding scholar," Caroline sang out. "The girl who will certainly bring pride to the school." Quoting the principal's speech—which she was sure Miss Maxwell had written.

Her father came into the kitchen from the other part of the house. He wasn't usually home at this hour.

"Fifty dollars!" she continued recklessly. "Miss Maxwell says tuition for the first year of university is $180, plus incidentals. Tomorrow she's going to help me apply for a bursary. And I'm going to write a letter to Bigwin Inn about a job...."

Her father broke in sharply. "Call your sisters for supper."

She hurried to the foot of the stairs and yelled, "Barb, Peggy, time for supper!"

When she got back to the kitchen, her father was heading out the door and the prize money was gone from the table.

"That's mine!" she shouted after him.

He didn't let on he heard.

She caught up with him as he opened his car door. "That's mine!" She grabbed his arm. He shoved her away. She grabbed harder, he shoved harder, sending her sprawling to the ground, from where she watched him get into his car and drive away.

Her mother watched from the kitchen door. "You little fool," she said. "You should've known better than to let him know you had it."

The next day Miss Maxwell asked what Caroline planned to do with the money. "You should open a bank account, you know. Don't leave it lying about."

Caroline was mortified, but told her what had happened.

Miss Maxwell was livid. "That man's a thief," she fumed. "He should be reported to the police!"

For one awful moment Caroline was afraid she was going to do just that.

But Miss Maxwell merely shook her head, opened her purse, withdrew her chequebook and filled out a cheque. She handed it to Caroline. "Pay me whenever you have money to spare."

The cheque was for fifty dollars.

Before Caroline could thank her, she asked. "How are you getting home?"

Caroline had stayed after school to fill out an application for a bursary so she'd missed the school bus. "I can walk."

"I'll drive you."

They didn't say much on the way. The backroads were narrow, unpaved and bumpy. It seemed to take all Miss Maxwell's concentration to keep her small car on the road. It was dusk by the time they arrived. She leaned across to open the door for Caroline, glancing up at the house. The small white frame house still in need of paint, the verandah still sloping to one side. The cat watched from the porch railing, the dog barked inside. Almost immediately a light came on over the kitchen door, the screen door slammed, and the dog came bounding towards the car.

"Mum must've heard us," Caroline said, ashamed of how

shabby the place looked, ashamed of the dog, ashamed of feeling this way.

Miss Maxwell planted a sad, dry kiss on her cheek. "It's time you got out of here, you do know that, don't you?"

The night her brothers finally let her father have it, she was in Toronto, living in St. Anne's residence for girls. Not all the girls were rich, some were daughters of men who worked for the government or taught in high schools, but most—like Miss Maxwell—wore their hair short. St. Anne's itself was like a little bit of England. An ivy-covered building built around a courtyard, with casement windows, heavy dark oak furniture, leather chairs and sofas. An oak-panelled library with portraits of past deans on the walls. The girls wore long black academic gowns over their clothes, the kind of gowns usually worn only at graduation.

Each evening they were expected to gather in the common room to play bridge or chat while they waited for the dean to lead them into dinner. "Shall we dine?" she'd flutter, a tall, skinny woman with a shock of white hair and Miss Maxwell's voice. The food was tasteless, but served with an elaborate array of cutlery, crystal, china and white linen. After dinner they returned to the common room for coffee and music. Classical music. Schubert Lieder or Bartok percussion suites. Later, upstairs in their rooms, the girls perched on their beds discussing love, sex, religion, art, work and their families.

Others did. Caroline never said a word about her family, although they were always with her. When her roommate Sally mentioned an older brother studying at Cambridge, she thought of Jim and Al living in a boarding-house, working in a factory. When Sally complained her mother had insisted she take ballet and piano lessons, she pictured Flo sitting in the kitchen, listening to her radio plays.

One morning she skipped classes and stayed in her room to write an overdue essay. The school janitor walked beneath the window, whistling a tune her father whistled. She was swept by feelings of love and sadness. After that the janitor took her father's place in her dreams; when her father started drinking again, in her dreams it was the janitor who fell off the wagon.

But it was guilt, not love, that prompted her to go home that weekend. She hadn't been for months. She hated the long bus ride, the cold dark lonely countryside. She hated the high dusty seats, the foggy windows, the sound of passengers snoring in air too stale to breathe. With each mile her resentment grew. She got off at Queen's Corners, then walked down the sideroad, the ground hard beneath her feet, the sky above dark and starry.

The minute she stepped inside the house, she knew something was wrong. Her brothers were home for the weekend but the house was deathly quiet, her mother nowhere in sight.

"Where's Mum?"

Nobody said a word.

"What's the matter?"

"Are you sure you want to know?" Her sister Barb now sixteen, had quit school but was still living at home; she knew exactly how long it was since Caroline had been home.

"Of course."

Barb was sitting in Flo's chair. She lit a cigarette, inhaled deeply, then rocked back and forth. "Dad came home last night drunk as usual." She glanced at Jim and Al who were sitting at the table, playing gin rummy. But they didn't look up, didn't let on they heard what she was saying. "He said he wanted his supper. Same old story. Mum was in bed. Jim told him he could make his own damn supper."

Caroline looked at Jim, Jim looked at Al.

"Dad knocked the crutches out from under Jim." Barb shrugged. "Al jumped him."

The moment, Caroline thought, they'd been waiting for all their lives.

Barb stood up. "I need an ashtray." She motioned for Caroline to follow her through the dining room to the hallway where they sat side by side on the stairs.

"Jesus," Barb said. "I've never seen anything like it. They got him down on the floor, beat the shit out of him. They punched his face, kicked him. Jim hit him with his crutches." She shook her head. "There was blood all over the place."

Caroline could think of nothing to say.

"When it was over, Dad went outside and sat in the yard, leaning up against the tree. He called me, told me I'd better phone the doctor, something was wrong, he couldn't breathe. I thought he was going to die." She folded her arms across her chest, rocking back and forth.

"What was Mum doing all this time?" asked Caroline.

Barb glanced toward the front of the house, her voice harder. "Mum? Mum became hysterical, screaming at Al and Jim, 'What have you done? How could you?'"

Caroline thought of all the times Jim and All had promised to do precisely this.

Barb took another drag on her cigerette. "It took the doctor an hour to get here. He said Dad's nose and ribs were broken, he'd had a heart attack. Told him to go to bed, he'd drop by later." She nodded in the direction of the spare bedroom off the living room. "They're in there."

Caroline walked to the door of the bedroom. Her father was lying on his back, his face turned towards the wall. Her mother sat by his side, holding his hand. She waited, but Flo didn't let on she knew Caroline was there.

"Mum?"

She didn't answer, didn't turn her head. Caroline walked back to the hallway. Barb had gone back to the kitchen and was sitting at the table watching Al and Jim play.

"She won't speak to any of us," Barb smiled grimly. "Nice, eh. Have you eaten?"

"I'm not hungry."

"Do you want a beer?"

"No."

Al laid down his cards; silently Jim gathered them up, shuffled, and began to deal again.

Caroline sat down at the table with them, wondering if Al and Jim realized that if their Dad died, they could be up for manslaughter.

Over the next couple of days, Flo floated in and out of the spare bedroom, closing the door behind her, never a glance in their direction. They'd become the enemy, their father the good guy, the man she'd fallen in love with.

When the doctor dropped by again they heard him say, "You're going to pull through this time. But you've got to stop drinking. It could happen again any time, your heart is in very bad shape."

Three and a half years later, Caroline graduated from St. Anne's with honours. On a beautiful, clear, sunny day. She looked around, hoping against hope she wouldn't run into Miss Maxwell. She'd never been back to see her, never repaid the money she owed her.

She couldn't do it. She just couldn't do it. Anymore than she could ask her father to return the fifty dollars he'd taken.

The courtyard was crowded with graduates, friends and families. At first she thought no one from her family was going to turn up. But there they were. Her father once more lean and healthy in his grey suit and a wide-brimmed fedora, looking like a rich American at an English tea-party. He had started a company selling a bookkeeping system to small shopkeepers and had more customers than he could handle. Flo stood next to him, clutching a new mink stole. Barb, who was now working for him, wore a simple black dress and beige jacket, her long dark hair combed forward over one eye, her mouth a bright patch of red. She had brought along her boyfriend Bud, a photographer with one of the city's biggest newspapers.

"I wouldn't've missed this for the world," her father said, handing Caroline a huge bouquet of roses. Bigger than any of the bouquets carried by the other girls. "Bud's going to take a picture of you for the weekend paper. I want the men at the office to see it."

"Smile, kiddo," Bud said, pushing his hat to the back of his head, his tie loose.

"Hold your flowers up," Flo said. "And straighten your hair."

We're making too much fuss, Caroline thought, running a hand through her hair, which was now cut short. She glanced around the courtyard. Other families stood in relaxed, happy groups, looking as if they'd done it all before. That was when she spotted Miss Maxwell, standing among the St. Anne's alumnae, watching her.

She could feel her cheeks burning.

Miss Maxwell smiled enigmatically, her gaze shifting from Caroline to her father.

"Smile," Bud called again. "Great," he said, and the camera clicked.

Judge

The weatherman was predicting a brutally hot summer. Hot and steamy. Jo-Anne decided to tackle the garden while it was still relatively cool.

The garden had been Richard's territory. He had filled it with perennials—crocusses, scillae, daffodils, narcissus, tulips—to which, each spring, he added dahlias and gladioli. The tulips had already bloomed but, with Richard gone, the dahlia and gladioli beds were empty. Jo-Anne had planted a few bleeding heart and violets in the corner by the kitchen; these had grown like weeds. She decided to coax them around the garden.

With a sharp spade she scooped up a clump of roots and carried them to the bed Richard had reserved for gladioli, picturing the yard the way it looked when they bought the house. A tangle of weeds, crab grass, rambling roses, an overgrown spirea, shaded by two huge sumacs. Richard had cut down the sumac—he wanted sun, he wanted flowers—replenished the soil, resodded the grass, and planted a magnolia tree, two lilac bushes, and more roses. The magnolia tree was now quite magnificent, the lilacs almost as high, and the rambling roses would soon burst across the back porch. Vibrant clusters of deep red. "They're like fireworks," her mother had exclaimed the previous summer.

Remembering this, Jo-Anne felt a twinge of guilt. She'd avoided her mother since Richard left, not wanting to hear, *I knew something like this was bound to happen.* Or worse still, *I will be praying for you.* Meaning praying they'd get back together.

Her mother's piety had always enraged Richard. Jo-Anne didn't blame him. In fact, in a perverse way his anger pleased her. She'd never felt close to her mother. Never felt loved by her. Nothing she did seemed to please her. "What a clever girl!" or "What a beautiful girl," her mother would say about Jo-Anne's friends. Never Jo-Anne herself. Once Jo-Anne was safely married and they'd adopted Mark and Amy, her mother had mellowed. But with Richard gone, she'd probably be more critical than ever.

Sighing, Jo-Anne went inside and made a list of bushes and vines she wanted for the garden: forsythia, holly, euonymus, English ivy and Virginia creeper to cover the fence. And a tree. She had asked Richard to plant a tree outside the kitchen window—a mountain ash—but he didn't think the neighbours would like it. Besides, he said, it would cut out a lot of sun. At the time, she felt she couldn't argue. But now the garden was her territory.

Jo-Anne phoned and asked Caroline for a lift to the nearest garden nursery. At times like this she was sorry she had stopped driving. She'd learned so she could take Mark and Amy to their swimming lessons, get them to a hospital in case of emergency, pick up groceries. But she'd never driven all that much; it had never seemed a natural thing for her to do. When he left, Richard took the car with him. In a way it had always been his.

The nursery was crowded with weekend gardeners—solitary men and women, enthusiastic couples, an elderly man and his gardener. Caroline helped Jo-Anne choose the plants on her list. Together they piled them on a trolley and headed for the trees. A beautiful flowering crab caught Caroline's eye. "Look at that!" she said. "Wouldn't you love to look out your window and see that every morning?"

"It is lovely," Jo-Anne said uncertainly.

Caroline checked the price tag. "It's half the price of a mountain ash." Caroline had no trouble making decisions.

"I'll take it."

When could she expect delivery? The next day, the salesman replied, unless of course she wanted it planted. Saturday was the soonest they could do that. Jo-Anne figured she and Mark could handle the bushes but a tree, no. "Saturday will be fine." She handed him her Visa. He handed her a small stake to mark the spot where the tree was to go.

First thing Saturday morning she drove the stake into the ground beneath the kitchen window, then walked to the corner for a carton of milk, eyeing her neighbours' trees along the way. One of them was a flowering crab. No longer flowering. Its foliage dark and dense and not very attractive. Dismal, oppressive.

Why had she never noticed it? She must have passed it a million times. She certainly wouldn't want to look out her window and see that every morning.

She raced home.

A truck was parked in her driveway and two men were unloading the flowering crab.

"Wait!" she shouted. "There's been a mistake."

The older of the two, a burly grey-haired man, began to flip through the pages of his order book.

"I mean, I've changed my mind." She smiled apologetically. "I'd like to exchange it."

He cast his eyes upward. "The office would have to authorize that, lady."

Jo-Anne got the feeling she was the first person, ever, to return a tree. Nevertheless she went inside and telephoned the nursery. She burbled on about the flowering crab on her neighbour's lawn, told them how long she had wanted a tree outside her kitchen window, how important it was to her. That she had intended to buy a mountain ash, but her neighbour had persuaded her to change her mind. Wearily, they agreed to take it back. Could she come that day to choose a replacement?

"They said I can exchange it."

The driver shrugged. "It's their decision."

"I don't suppose there's room in the truck for a passenger," she asked brightly.

An awkward silence.

"I can ride in the back," his helper volunteered—a young man, friendly—and leapt in next to the tree.

The driver got in behind the wheel, leaving Jo-Anne to open the passenger door herself. As she stepped up into the cab, she was hit by the smell of tobacco and stale sweat. The motor was already running. The driver leaned across to make sure she had closed the door properly, then took off down the street. He turned the corner, drove to the nearest intersection, right, left, then headed north on the parkway. Not a word.

"I'm going to change it for a mountain ash," Jo-Anne said, breaking the silence. "Such beautiful lacy trees!"

"They don't last long," he said evenly, his eyes fixed firmly on the road. "Maybe six years."

Jo-Anne thought about this. "My neighbour has had a mountain ash in his garden for years. I'm sure it's been more than six years."

"He's lucky." He began to whistle.

Oh God, Jo-Anne thought. What do I know about gardening. I should have hired a landscape gardener, or at least consulted one. "If you were buying a tree," she asked finally, "What would you choose?"

"A skyline locust." He turned and looked at her. "They're bred to withstand acid rain."

So that's what she got. The biggest one on the lot. She'd waited ten years, she wasn't going to wait another ten years for it to grow. When the tree was firmly in the ground, the men gone, she poured herself a glass of white wine and sat in the late afternoon sun admiring its lacy foliage and, in a way, herself. I've done it, she thought, I've really done it.

Somewhere a phone was ringing. She hurried inside. It was Sheila, her elder sister. "What are you doing?"

"Gardening."

"Why don't you come up to the cottage for the rest of the weekend. David will pick you up."

"Well, actually, I'm enjoying myself."

Sheila laughed. "Suit yourself. It's an open invitation. Come any weekend you're at loose ends."

The phone rang again almost instantly. It was Caroline.

"What are you doing?"

"Gardening."

"Come and have a drink with us. Steve just dropped by with a friend."

Steve was Caroline's recent lover, a cameraman. His friend Judge is a short intense man with dark skin and large luminous eyes. An Indian educated in Dehli and Oxford. He studied history intending to become a teacher, he tells them, but changed his mind. "It's the present that interests me. The legacy of the past. Making documentary films allows me to explore both." He's just finished a film about historic gardens and does a little landscape gardening on the side.

"What a coincidence," Caroline says, "Jo-Anne is remodelling her garden."

Judge is interested. Jo-Anne, embarrassed.

"Caroline, you know I'm not a gardener.... I'm just trying to fix up the yard."

Judge offers to inspect what she has done.

Jo-Anne shows him the English Ivy she hopes will eventually cover the wall at the bottom of the garden.

"Cover the wall? You'll need many more plants," Judge says briskly. "At least five."

She shows him the spirea she has planted in the corner behind the gate.

"Oh, it will never grow there," Judge says. "It needs six square feet. Plant it here."

He thinks the Virgina Creeper will look just fine along the east fence but suggests she add clematis. "Mix them up. Virginia creeper and clematis."

"What a good idea." Why hadn't she thought of that? Her mother has always loved clematis. And Rose of Sharon.

"And how about some Boston Ivy on the side of the garage.

To take the edge off."

Richard wouldn't like that. "A good idea."

Judge casts a final glance around the yard; he doesn't seem to notice the tree. "How do you like the tree?" Jo-Anne prods.

"Did you just plant it? Such a large tree? Well, it looks healthy. The shape is good." His eyes slide over the fence to her neighbour's mountain ash. "That's a pretty tree."

Jo-Anne's throat tightens. "Do you think a mountain ash would have been better?"

"No, no the locust is fine."

Relieved, she invites him in for a drink. Her teenage children are rummaging in the kitchen for something to eat.

"Why don't I make dinner for all of us," Jo-Anne suggests.

"Why don't we go out for dinner?" Judge says. "I know a nice little Greek restaurant, not too far."

"It won't take me a minute to whip something up..."

Her son Mark looks embarrassed. "Mum, go on," he says.

Over dinner Jo-Anne and Judge talk about their marriages. His wife has left him for a friend from India, a younger friend. "Can you imagine how that feels, can you?"

Jo-Anne says she thinks she can.

"What happened to you?"

"Something similar." Which isn't exactly true. Richard is seeing someone—a colleague from the university, a carefree, confident woman—but that started after he left. "I think someone else might make you happy," was the reason he gave when he suggested they spend some time apart. She has no doubt his colleague will make him happy. Has made him happy. She sighs.

Judge reaches for her hand. A gesture of sympathy, but it doesn't stop there. His hand lingers, holding hers in a warm masculine grasp. Something deep inside her unfolds.

"I'm leaving for Vancouver in the morning. I'll be back next weekend. I'll call you when I'm back," he tells her. "We can spend some time together then."

He kisses her goodnight on the doorstep. A long, sweet kiss

she feels to her toes. It still works, she thinks gratefully, the magic still works. She undresses and crawls into bed a happy woman, enjoying the feel of the sheets against her thighs, her back, her breasts, her hips. Still there.

But when she wakes, it's Richard she longs for. She can't live without him. She can't manage without him. The house, the children, her work, the garden.

The garden.

In the kitchen, she hurries to the window; her tree is still standing. It is a pretty tree, a very pretty tree. She reaches for the phone and dial's her sister Sheila's number. "Does that invitation still hold?"

"Of course. When do you want to come?"

"Next weekend. If that's all right."

"It's fine. Will you bring Mark and Amy with you?"

"No. They're going to spend a few weeks with Richard."

"Well, Mum will be here."

"Oh." Jo-Anne's heart sinks.

"It'll be fine," Sheila says. "David will pick you up."

Jo-Anne spends the day swimming with Sheila. Their mother sits on the deck or takes Sheila's two young grandchildren for a walk, telling them stories from her childhood. She's so much easier with them, Jo-Anne thinks. There had been no hugging and kissing when she and Sheila were small.

Her mother is sitting on the deck now, in a pale blue dress, white sweater over her shoulders, a straw hat to shield her skin from the sun. Ankles crossed, one hand on her lap, the other at her throat. A Victorian gesture of modesty. She looks so tiny, Jo-Anne thinks. And so old. She doesn't usually think of her mother as old, but of course she is.

Saturday night the adults play Scrabble, the children Monopoly. Later, in the kitchen, Jo-Anne and Sheila make hot chocolate for the children.

"Mother is a lot less critical than she used to be, have you noticed?" Jo-Anne remarks. There had been no talk about Jo-

Anne's marriage. No suggestion she had failed in any way.

"A lot less."

"Remember all that talk about sin, the redeeming power of Jesus?"

Sheila smiles. "Mother lost interest in Jesus when Dad died. I'm surprised you didn't notice that." She places mugs on a tray. "Besides she's almost eighty. People seem to become more tolerant as they grow older." She turns to Jo-Anne. "Are you in a hurry to get back?"

"No...."

"Then why don't you stay up for a few days. Just the two of you. I have to be in town, but David can come up for you."

"Oh I'm not sure I want to do that."

Monday morning Jo-Anne wakes to the sound of her mother puttering in the kitchen. This, she realizes, is the first time she's spent days alone with her mother. Growing up, there was always a brother or sister around. Later, her own children. She sits up and looks out the window. The sky is clear, the lake smooth.

"Mother," she calls. "I'm going for a swim."

"Don't go out too far," her mother calls back. "Swim along the shore."

The cottages on either side are empty, a single sailboat skims along the horizon. The lake is luminous, turquoise near the beach, deep blue at the end of the dock. Gingerly, Jo-Anne steps into the water; it's almost warm. She swims out past the dock then turns on her side and swims parallel to the shore. Willows trail in the water, a wild canary darts among the branches, a blackbird struts along the beach. She turns and floats on her back, as carefree as a child. A single white cloud drifts above her.

When she steps out of the water, her mother is standing at the screen door, watching. Smiling, Jo-Anne hurries across the lawn and grabs her towel from the deck. "The water's beautiful!"

Her mother holds open the door then turns and leads the way inside the cottage.

Breakfast is on the table, the kind of breakfast her mother

always made: orange juice, toast and tea, a soft-boiled egg. "Sit by the window," she tells Jo-Anne. "I'll sit here." Meaning the chair nearest the teapot. Jo-Anne holds out her cup, offering in return a description of the wild canary she has seen. "It looked just like the canary Aunt Fay had for so long."

Her mother's eyes soften. "Do you remember Pete?"

"Of course."

Pete was her mother's pet budgie. *Pretty Pete, Pretty Pete,* she called him, talking to him as she moved about the kitchen. When her work was done, she'd open his cage and let him fly around the house. "I just can't bear to see him cooped up all day."

How she loved that bird.

Inevitably, someone left a window open. They searched for days, calling *Pretty Pete, Pretty Pete,* up and down nearby streets, in and out of open garages, under porches. Her mother paid the neighbours' children to call his name under every tree within blocks.

Her mother sighs. "I often wonder what happened to him." She curls her hands around the warmth of her cup and looks out the window at the surrounding trees.

"Mum," Jo-Anne says gently. "I'll do the dishes, then we'll go for a nice long walk."

"You go ahead. I want to tidy up."

She wants to keep house, Jo-Anne thinks, make beds, dust, sweep the floor, the way she used to.

Well, that too is a form of love.

When everything is in order, her mother sits outside on the deck, a book open on her lap, staring out at the lake. "It reminds me of when your father was alive."

Jo-Anne's father built the cottage fifteen years before he died. Her mother had fought him every inch of the way. *It's too big. It's too expensive. The layout is impractical.* Yet, once it was finished, she enjoyed it, spending summers there long after he died, long after she could manage on her own, long after the family had gone their separate ways and wanted her to sell it. She refused.

Her father was seventy-two when he died, but Jo-Anne remembers a younger man. Standing in the water to repair the dock. Kneeling to make sure the children's lifejackets were fastened. At the helm of the boat, pointing to something on the horizon. Always busy. The only time he seemed to sit still was in the evening, reading the newspaper. As a child she had loved to sit on his knee, helping him turn the pages. He'd tell her when, stopping occasionally to rub his whiskers against her cheek.

Toward the middle of the week, the sky clouds over, a wind blows out of nowhere, the temperature drops. Jo-Anne makes dinner while her mother naps, and after dinner reads while her mother listens to the radio. The minute the program is over, her mother says "It's time for bed." Jo-Anne, who has been having trouble sleeping since Richard left, falls asleep as soon as her head hits the pillow.

A thunderstorm wakes her. The tree outside her window sways ominously. The light she left burning in the hallway flickers and goes out. She hurries to the kitchen and rummages for a candle but almost immediately the electricity comes back on, the storm settling into a noisy downpour.

Her mother too was wakened by the storm. She was awake for most of the night, she tells Jo-Anne next morning.

"You must be exhausted."

But her mother doesn't look tired, she looks peaceful. "I felt as if you were all here."

"What do you mean, all of us?"

"The family."

"Even Dad?"

"All of you."

Their last morning together, Jo-Anne sprawls on a deck with a book. Her mother calls from the cottage.

"Jo-Anne, would you do something for me?"

Jo-Anne sits up and closes her book. "Of course."

"Would you wash my hair?" Her mother smiles apologetically. "I'm getting too old to do that."

Jo-Anne hurries inside. Her mother is sitting at the kitchen table, her bathrobe loosened from her shoulders, leaning over a basin of warm water. There's a ladle next to it, a tube of shampoo, and a towel over the back of her chair.

Jo-Anne pours water over her hair then rubs it with the shampoo. The physical closeness, the intimacy, startles her. Her mother's shoulders are so small, so frail, her flesh so soft and white. So mortal. This is the woman my father loved, she thinks. The woman who gave me life. An inexpressible tenderness wells up inside her.

She rinses her mother's hair again and again, until the last traces of shampoo are gone. "There, it's done." she says, wrapping a towel around her mother's head.

Her mother pulls her bathrobe up around her shoulders. "Thank you."

"Mum, do you love me?" Jo-Anne asks suddenly, startling both of them.

"Of course I love you, we all love you." But her mother's eyes are stricken. "I wasn't a very good mother."

"Of course you were a good mother."

She shakes her head. "No, I didn't show affection."

"Oh Mum." Jo-Anne puts her arms around her. "Nobody showed affection then. Nobody."

At home, Jo-Anne finds a note from Caroline, who was looking after the house while she was away. She hopes everything is okay. *Someone named Judge called several times and seemed very upset not to be able to reach you.* Jo-Anne rummages through the mail. There it is, a postcard from Vancouver. On the back he has written, *That was a great evening. You're great. We'll have many more.* Judge.

A nice man, she thinks. A very nice man. She hopes he'll call again, but she doesn't regret what she has done.

She hurries to inspect her garden. It has rained here too. The leaves are green, the earth moist. Sun catches the upper branches of her tree. It seems to have grown while she was away. Several birds are perched on a lower branch, as if the tree has always been there. Next year she'll plant another. A birch maybe. And a Rose of Sharon. Why not?

My Husband's Wedding

Liz woke with that awful what time is it, what day is it feeling. She lay on her bed, fully clothed, the room in darkness except for the light from the street. The park across the way empty. She'd had a glass of wine with dinner then gone upstairs to read. Katy must still be out.

The telephone rang. It was Brian.

"It's me. I must talk to you."

The moment she heard his voice, she knew what he was going to say. "You're getting married."

"Yes," he said. "Next week. On the 9th." As if it was all her fault.

"Why didn't you tell me sooner?" she said, trying to sound like a busy woman with more important things on her mind.

"We just decided on the date."

'We' was recent. For a long time after he moved in with Terri, he'd gone on talking like a man who lived alone. *I'm going to do this, I'm too busy for that, I really don't know what my plans are.* Which was irritating. 'We' was worse.

"I think you and I should meet," he said.

"Brian, I'm not going to sit around discussing your wedding. Just tell me where you want the kids, and when."

"I really don't think it concerns them," he said.

"You don't think it *concerns* them?" She sat up. "They're your children. Terri will be their stepmother." Terri was twelve years older than their son Sam, fifteen years older than Katy.

"Terri will not be their stepmother." His voice rose, as it did when he was angry.

"She will, Brian," Liz goaded quietly.

"She will not." There would be no messy spillover from his life with Liz into his new marriage.

"I have to go," Another minute and she'd be screaming at him, how can you do this to them?

"We've got to make plans for the summer. It would be easier face to face," Brian said.

They rarely met face to face. Liz had decided early on she wasn't going to do that. Five minutes in his emotional field, as she now thought of it, and she fell apart.

"I'm very busy, Brian."

"I could come by the house."

The house. Their house. "No, I'll meet you somewhere," Liz said.

"For lunch?"

"All right."

"Where?"

Where? "The Viscount." The restaurant they used to go to after family therapy the summer Sam got in trouble. Surely the proximity of all those social workers would keep her on track.

"When?"

"One o'clock."

"Try to be on time," he said coolly and hung up.

Bastard, she thought, slamming down the receiver. He's going through with it. He's really going to marry that girl. She had begun to hope it wouldn't happen, that he'd move on to someone else, someone older, plainer, fatter. Someone who'd had nothing to do with the break-up of their marriage. Someone she could talk to about the kids. She should never have agreed to a no-fault divorce. It was all too quick.

She heard Katy come in downstairs. "I'm up here Katy," she called out.

Katy came pounding up the stairs. "Were you on the phone?"

"How did you know?"

Katy searched her face. "Have you been crying? " she asked angrily.

"No, of course not."

"Who was it? "

"Your Dad."

"What did he want?" Katy suspected her parents were plotting again. She had complained to Liz recently that her life was worse than anyone's she knew. Her dog had died, her brother had gone away to boarding school, and her father had left. Now something else, something really awful, was going to happen. She knew it.

"He just wanted to talk to me," Liz said, trying to sound casual.

"What about?"

"The summer."

Katy looked skeptical. Liz tried another tack.

"How was the movie?"

"I don't want to talk about it."

What she meant was that she didn't want Liz analyzing her feelings about the movie. She hated all that ikey-psychy stuff. Liz blamed herself for this. Shortly after Brian left, in a fit of anxiety she had taken Katy to a family clinic for assessment. She waited downstairs while Katy was interviewed upstairs by a couple of young psychologists in training. Did Katy ever hear voices when there was no one else in the room, they asked, enunciating clearly, their voices gentle, their smiles encouraging. No, Katy told them. Did she ever think she saw things out of the corner of her eye, but when she looked, there was nothing there? No, she said. They decided to level with her. Your mother is very worried about you. You know that don't you? Katy said she did. She supposed that was why her mother was with her. Your mother is with you? Yes. They exchanged glances. Your mother is *here* with you? Yes. They wrote furiously, thinking they'd struck pure gold. My mother is downstairs, Katy said impatiently. She told Liz later she thought they were nuts.

"Do you want a cup of hot chocolate?" Liz asked.

"No."

"There's some fruit yogurt and cookies."

"I don't want anything."

Katy walked into her own room, closing the door firmly behind her. Liz heard her television start. She watches too damn much junk, she thought, but didn't have the heart to say anything. I must do something special for her birthday, she told herself. Something different. The year before—their first without Brian—Katy had insisted they celebrate exactly as they always did: tea in bed in the morning with special treats while she opened her presents. Brian's idea originally, he loved birthdays. They might as well have poured a cup of tea for him.

Liz decided to take the morning off work, she wanted lots of time to dress. She didn't want Brian wondering what he'd ever seen in her. "You've let yourself go terribly," was what her mother said after Brian left her, but she'd lost twenty pounds since then, bought a lot of new clothes, and had a few facials. Her first appointment the beautician asked if she was divorced. Liz was startled. "How can you tell?" The beautician smiled. "Most of my clients are." I've become a walking cliche, Liz thought, but made another appointment.

By her third treatment, her friends were telling her she looked better than she had in years, relaxed as well as slender. "The bones are showing in your face again," was how one friend put it. Thanks to her bones, Liz looked younger than she was.

She changed three times before she found what she wanted to wear: a new skirt and top, soft and flowing, not too formal, not too casual, something Brian had never seen.

She brushed a little pink of her cheeks. Brian hated rouge. At the beautician's suggestion, she had also begun to use a little colour on her hair. Not enough to completely cover the grey. Certainly not. Just enough to give it life.

Liz had trouble leaving the house at the best of times. Sometimes the simple act of closing the door, putting the key in the lock filled her with dread—she would come home and find the house burned to the ground, the cat inside. She went back in and checked the stove, the iron, made sure the back door was locked, then hurried to the corner, a wide and windy intersection, a terrible place on a cold day. She decided to take a taxi. Five minutes passed. A cab cruised by in the opposite direction. And then another. Liz waved her arms and hollered, "Taxi! Taxi!", which she hated doing, but the driver didn't stop. She hurried across the street. A taxi sped by the corner she'd just left and then while she debated what to do, another. I am going to be late, she thought. Brian will be furious. I'll phone the Viscount, tell them to say I had to rush the cat to the vet's. Just then a taxi pulled up in front of her.

Brian was waiting outside the Viscount. Wearing the expensive grey tweed jacket he'd bought the spring they separated. The one that matched his hair. A good looking man, distinguished, fit. She'd forgotten just how good looking. Only his eyes looked tired.

"Hello, Elizabeth."

Oh Christ, she thought, we might as well be standing here naked. The predisposition to love—*here is the man I want to be the centre of my life, here is the man I want to take charge of my life*—she'd felt it the first time she saw him, she felt it whenever he returned after a long absence, old scores swept away, the possibility of a new start, she felt it now, briefly, like the flicker of a burnt-out lightbulb.

"Sorry I'm late," she said. "Katy's school phoned just as I was leaving." Katy's school had phoned, that much was true.

The waiter led them to their usual table. "I haven't seen you two in a long time. How're Sam and Katy?"

"Sam's fine," Liz replied, thinking how nice of him to remember. "Still a handful but okay. It's Katy's who's having a bit of...."

"They're both fine," Brian interrupted sharply. His look forbade any discussion of their children, his children, with a waiter, however friendly. "Do you know what you want?" he asked.

Liz wanted to hit him. She wanted to tell the waiter, it's very kind of you to ask. Don't mind him, he's like that. The anger felt good. God, she thought, I wouldn't go back to our marriage for anything.

She ordered a salad.

Brian ordered a Reuben sandwich and coffee.

Liz remembered that Terri didn't drink and ordered a glass of wine. She leaned back against the seat and looked around. The Viscount was a fifties-style restaurant whose time had come again. It was crowded, noisy. Men and women in their thirties and forties, casually dressed in expensive leathers and imported cottons, laughed easily, exchanging confidences. No longstanding couples here. No children.

Brian leaned forward, getting down to business. "I'm going west for a couple of months. We're opening an office in Edmonton."

Good, she thought, they're having a working honeymoon. Nothing's changed.

"It means of course that I won't be seeing the children on weekends."

"Of course," she smiled sweetly.

Brian glared.

He had insisted on joint custody, the right to see them every weekend, all summer long, but it was taken for granted that she would be there to look after them when he had other more pressing or more interesting plans. Which of course is the way it had been all along. Why had she thought a separation agreement would change that?

"How are they doing in school?" he asked.

"Not great. I'm really worried about Katy. Afraid she might fail her year."

"You know my feelings about that."

His feelings were that it was all Liz's fault. She was programming Katy to fail, she was programming both children to fail, to get back at him for leaving her to raise them on her own. He had actually said this to her, in so many words.

The waiter brought their lunch.

"Katy's teachers are concerned about her too. I suppose you think they're programming her to fail."

"I wouldn't be surprised."

"Oh what's the use," Liz said angrily, picking the black olives out of her salad. "You wanted to talk about plans for the summer?"

"Yes." He patted his mouth with his napkin and laid it on the table. "We'll move up to the cottage as soon as we get back. I'll take Katy with me as usual but I think Sam should go to camp. I don't want to have to deal with him."

Liz put down her fork. "Sam will be terribly upset!" Sam hated camp and loved the cottage. In some ways it was more like home than their house in town. They'd spent their best and worst times there. Liz ordered another glass of wine.

"I really think you should know my plans." Brian said, shoving a piece of paper across the table. On it he had scribbled the dates of his marriage and honeymoon. He was getting married on the ninth. On the tenth he and Terri were going to Montreal for a brief honeymoon before heading west.

"You're not serious?"

Brian and Liz had met in Montreal. They had spent weekends eating, drinking and making love in her apartment. Her wonderful, big, romantic apartment. As far as she knew he had no other connection with the city. For one crazy moment she thought, they're going to spend their honeymoon in my old apartment! It's not enough to end our marriage, he has to go back and relive it with her. Oh shit, I'm going to cry. She got to her feet, fumbling in her purse for her sunglasses. "I'll get back to you."

A taxi was right outside. She blurted her address to the driver then sobbed all the way home. Once inside, she called Caroline. "How can he do this to me, to them?" she wailed.

"It's the act of an insane man," Caroline replied calmly.

"Do you want me to come over?"

"No," Liz said, blowing her nose. "I have to go to work."

Work was doing research for a small educational film and video company. Caroline had got her the job. The office was at the north end of the subway, away from downtown, so she could always count on a seat. Normally she loved the long ride. Time to read or think or just daydream. She closed her eyes behind her sunglasses and leaned her head against the window, imagining what her mother would say when she heard about the wedding. I don't know what you're making so much fuss about, she'd say. You two weren't happy together, you were always complaining. Maybe that girl will make him happy.

One last tear began to slide down Liz's cheek. She lifted the frame of her glasses and with the back of her hand wiped the tear upward, as if it were something in her eye. A trick her brother had taught her when they were small.

The man across the aisle was watching her, concerned. An elderly man, with white hair and a pink face, dressed in clean pants and plaid shirt like a boy on his way to school. Liz smiled to let him know she was all right. What am I doing, she thought, upsetting such a sweet old man. Making a public spectacle of myself. What does it matter who Brian marries?

But it did matter.

She turned back to the window. What would Caroline say? Of course you're upset. It's one more nail in the coffin. But this too will pass. In time you'll think of Brian the way you think of your brothers, your father. In time Brian will become part of your history, your past.

The moment Liz stepped inside her office, she felt better. Stronger. Saner. The office was a cubbyhole really, but she loved it, it was her space. She had hung the walls with posters from the art gallery and the windowsill was crowded with plants: the rubber plant Sam had given her the Christmas before last, a Hibiscus plant she had bought herself, some spiky foliage left behind by her predecessor. Her bookcase was filled with sociology texts of one sort or another. On her desk newspaper clippings were arranged in order. She had no trouble being tidy here.

Home was a different matter. There were piles of clothes everywhere, books, mail, waiting to be put away. It was something she and Brian had fought about from the very beginning, what the self-help books called an anchor point. Something you have agreed to fight about.

Katy had told her Terri was obsessively tidy. She and Brian must have agreed to fight about other things. Helen, Brian's first wife, had been untidy too. He had said as much the first time she met him. She supposed Terri now heard what a terrible housekeeper she was. Which wasn't exactly true. She was an experienced interior decorator, even if she didn't want to do that anymore. She was good at the general effect—colour, pictures, the placement of furniture—but cleaning, tidying, no. Towards the end, of course, they had fought about everything. If she turned down the heat, he turned it up. If she told the kids it was time for bed, he said they could stay up a little longer. Or the other way round.

There was a note from her boss propped up against her phone. *I want to see you. Maeve.* Liz put the lid back on her coffee and continued along the hall.

"How would you like to go to Montreal?" Maeve leaned back in her chair, clasped her hands beneath her chin, and smiled.

"Montreal?"

"Yes," Maeve smiled. "Montreal." She knew Liz had lived in Montreal and was offering this trip as a reward for good work. "I want you to meet the woman who made the adoption film. See how you think she'd come across on TV. And talk to publicity about the housing film. Two days at most."

"When?"

"Next week. The ninth and tenth."

Liz stared at her, unbelieving..

"Something wrong?"

"I'm not sure I can leave the kids," Liz said finally.

"You've left them before."

"Not at a time like this."

"What's happening next week?"

"My husband's wedding," Liz grimaced. "Brian's getting married on the ninth."

"It won't last," Maeve said quickly. "She won't put up with him."

Maeve knew all about Brian and Terri. Right from the start, Maeve and Liz had talked about personal matters as well as work. Their houses, their children, their husbands. Maeve had a wonderful sense of humour, talking with her made Liz's difficulties with Brian seem hilarious. They would howl with laughter at the things he did and said. It wasn't surprising that Maeve took it for granted Liz would be glad to be rid of him. Which in one sense she was, but in another, deeper sense, she wasn't. What was funny at the office was not funny at home. And what was funny before Terri was definitely not funny after Terri.

"Are you all right?"

"I'm fine."

"Are you sure?"

"Positive."

Maeve looking skeptical. She was a handsome woman with bobbed white hair. A photograph of her family stood on her desk. Husband, tall sons and daughters, grandchildren, grouped in front of the family cottage. The wall behind her was hung with awards for films she had made. Her life is perfect, Liz thought, not for the first time. She stayed home with her children when they were small, went back to university when they no longer needed her, and carved a good career for herself. And she did it without losing her husband, without colouring her hair, without facials.

"You're sure you're all right?"

"I can't pretend it's a day like any other, but yes, I'm fine."

Maeve shook her head. "Marriages come and go, but divorce goes on forever."

Liz was still in bed when Brian arrived the next morning to take Katy to her riding lesson. The doorbell rang and rang.

"Katy answer it!" Liz hollered.

"You answer it," Katy hollered back.

"That'll be your dad."

"Tell him I'm almost ready."

Usually Liz stayed out of sight when Brian came to pick the

children up. They had gone through a period of trying to greet each other like friendly adults, but that had ended almost before it began. "Why don't you come in and wait," she had suggested one morning, like a schoolteacher welcoming a visiting parent.

"No I won't.... Well, yes I will. It's cold outside," he said smiling, his chin in the air, then followed her into the kitchen.

"A cup of tea?"

He shook his head, but almost immediately reconsidered that too. "Well, yes I will."

Liz poured him a cup, added milk and sugar, and put it on the kitchen table. "Won't you sit down?"

He hesitated."Well, why not."

She shooed the cat off a chair for him and he sat down, glancing at the familiar objects that lined the shelves: pots and pans he had used a million times, the antique Wearever juicer he had found in the country, the copper planter someone had given them as a wedding present. The cat began to rub around his ankles. He leaned down and patted it, with the look of someone who knows he's made a terrible mistake. The next time Liz invited him inside, he said no, he would wait in the car.

The doorbell sounded again.

"Mu-um, answer it!"

Reluctantly, Liz grabbed her robe and ran downstairs to the door. "Katy'll be down in a few minutes." The air felt cool and fresh. She tightened her robe around her. It was new, an expensive fine wool paisley. Bought to replace the old one of Brian's she'd been in the habit of wearing around the house.

"I do wish you'd make sure she's up on time," Brian said, noticing the gown.

"Why don't you call and wake her," she said evenly.

"In future, I will." He headed back toward the car.

Halfway down the walk, he turned. "By the way, my plans have changed. We won't be going to Montreal. I'm not sure what we'll be doing." He smiled distantly. "Someone told me Chicago's a terrific town."

"You always did have trouble with pleasure trips," Liz said

evenly. "Are you going to talk to Katy about the wedding?"

"I haven't decided."

"You know she should hear it from you. Have you talked to Sam?"

"I'll call him this weekend. In any case, there's not going to be a wedding in the sense you're talking about. We're going down to the city hall in the morning. We've invited a few people back for a reception later. It'll be an adult party. I don't think they'd enjoy it."

"Mabye you're right and maybe they won't want to go," she replied doggedly. "But you should give them the choice."

Katy came clattering down the stairs, long and leggy in her riding pants and boots, her hair still damp from the shower. Liz watched as she handed her crop and tack box to Brian then walked with him to the car. Her daddy's little princess as long as the day lasted. She wondered how long the riding lessons would last. Katy had dropped ballet when she took up riding. She had dropped piano when Brian was no longer there to praise her, though she played as naturally as most people breathe. "I have never taught a more talented child," her teacher had said.

Inside the phone was ringing. Liz hurried to answer it. It was Jennie, Brian's daughter from his first marriage, calling from London.

"Is he trying to replace me or what," Jennie said angrily. "She's my age." Jennie had just turned twenty-seven.

Liz said, "I'm not sure exactly how old she is."

"I asked him. She's twenty-eight and a half."

"Twenty-eight and a half?"

"Yes."

"He said that?" The kids used to say they were eight and a half, nine and a half, trying to make themselves sound older. But to talk about a grown woman being twenty-eight and a half....

"Yes." Jennie sounded upset.

"Jennie, it has nothing to do with you. You mustn't think that."

There was a moment of silence at the other end of the line.

"Jennie, are you there?"

"Does that mean he will start a third family?"

"Probably."

"Will that hurt?"

Liz couldn't answer that.

"Are you okay?"

"I'm fine."

"You know how much I love you."

"Oh Jennie, I love you too." Jennie had been part of her life for almost twenty years, travelling back and forth from London to Toronto to spend school breaks, summer holidays, Christmases. Liz had been afraid she might lose her along with Brian.

Sam called the following evening from boarding school. Brian had invited him to the wedding reception but he wasn't sure he wanted to go. "I asked him if I could live with them and he said no, there isn't room in their apartment."

Damn him. "Maybe they'll move into something bigger after the wedding." Silence at the other end. "Sam?"

"It's because of her. It isn't fair. He's known me all my life and he just met her."

"We'll talk about it when you're here. When are you coming?"

"Wednesday night."

"I'll pick you up at the bus station."

"Dad said he would."

Katy came running down the stairs just as Liz hung up. "Was that Sam?"

"Yes. He's coming home on Wednesday."

"Is he going?"

"You'll have to ask him."

"I'm not going if he's not going."

"That's up to you."

Liz began to tidy up the kitchen.

Katy watched her. "Do you know how embarrassing this is?" she said. "How would you like to have to tell your friends your dad is getting married?"

Liz said nothing, remembering an earlier time when Katy had asked, how would you like to tell your friends your dad has a girlfriend?

"Anybody home?" Sam tossed his bag on the chair inside the door. He was wearing torn jeans and his black leather jacket, now much too small for him but he refused to abandon it. He hated his school uniform, he hated his school. Katy got to him before Liz.

"Are you going?"

"I don't know. Are you?"

"I dunno. Who do you think will be there?"

Over dinner, Sam complained about Brian. "He told me to bring my dress clothes with me. 'You've got to dress properly'," he said imitating Brian, "'if you're coming to the reception'."

"Did you bring them?" Liz asked.

"Ya, but I'm not wearing them."

"What are you wearing?" Katy asked.

"My white pants and jacket."

His Miami Vice suit. Liz pictured him, black hair curling over his shoulders, turquoise shirt open at the neck. Sexy. She wondered how Brian would feel about that.

"Why don't you wear your Rasta hat," said Katy.

"Katy!" Liz said, then remembered that Katy had outgrown her party dress. "You'll need something new to wear to the wedding. We can go shopping tomorrow."

Katy shook her head. "If I go, I'll wear something of yours."

Liz didn't want her clothes going to the wedding.

"Katy, I really think...."

"He's such a hypocrite," Sam said. "Remember how he used to say age doesn't matter. Remember those drawings you did of that old woman?" he asked Liz.

"She wasn't old." Liz said firmly. She was in her late thirties. Younger than Liz.

"She was old and ugly and fat. Dad said she was beautiful," he sneered. "'Women can be beautiful at any age,' he said. Now he's marrying someone young enough to be his daughter."

"Maybe age has nothing to do with it," Liz said. "Maybe what he likes about Terri has nothing to do with age." I shouldn't have to do this, she thought.

"It was all a lot of bullshit," Sam snorted. "What would he think if I went out with a woman forty-three?"

Katy waited to hear what Liz would say.

"I've got to make a few phone calls. Sam, you clear the table and Katy, you stack the dishwasher." Damn him, she thought. Why doesn't he talk to Sam.

Upstairs in her room Liz sits by the window overlooking the park. Brian and Terri live in an expensive, fashionable hotel-apartment in the centre of town. Not very big according to the kids but with rooms to rent for receptions and parties. She supposes that's what they're going to do. She pictures Brian drawing up the guest list, planning the food, while Terri stands by, waiting to carry out instructions. As she did the day she and Brian got married. Terri, she is sure, is glad the waiting is over, confident she'll make Brian happy, that she'll succeed where Liz failed. As she'd thought she would succeed where Helen had failed.

The day of the wedding is chilly and overcast. A terrible day for a wedding, Liz thinks, pleased. Sam comes downstairs dressed in his white suit. Katy is wearing Liz's designer sweater and a long skirt.

"You both look very nice," Liz smiles. "What time are you supposed to be there?"

"Twelve-thirty."

She looks at her watch. "A quarter to." Brian and Terri are probably down at city hall this very moment.

"Can we take a taxi?"

"You can take a taxi. Are you sure you'll be all right on your own?"

Sam and Katy roll their eyes. "Mum, we're not children."

Liz watches them leave then pulls on a warm sweater, pours herself a cup of coffee and goes outside to sit on the deck. She wishes she'd made some plans. Invited Caroline and Jo-Anne for lunch. It's morbid sitting out here alone while Brian get's married. My husband's wedding.

The day of her wedding, hers and Brian's, had been a beautiful day. She'd bought a white lace Mexican dress, Brian wore his Indian whites and sandals. The latest in fashion then. He'd hung the deck with flowers and lanterns while she organized the food. They'd invited over eighty guests. It was a crazy, joyful day—despite her misgivings. She'd wanted a small reception.

"That's because you don't want to be married," Brian had teased, one Sunday morning in bed. "What difference will it make? We're married now," she countered, afraid of the difference it would make. "We're not married, we're living together," he said. They'd been living together for over a year, waiting for his divorce from Helen to come through. "Marriage means standing up in front of the world and saying we're going to live together for the rest of our lives. Till death do us part." He kissed her solemnly. "There will never be anyone else for me. Now let's have breakfast. The kind you used to make in Montreal." And he bounded out of bed to put some music on.

Now he eats breakfast with Terri, Liz thinks, and plays his music for her. And at some point this afternoon he will stand up in front of our friends, put his arms around her, and say, this is my wife, there will never be anyone else for me. It's not true. He can't possibly feel for Terri what he felt for me. Doesn't she know that? And then it hits her: Helen must have felt like this. She must have thought, Brian can't possibly feel for Liz what he felt for me.

Liz closes her eyes, realizing for the first time that on that crazy, joyful day she hadn't thought of Helen once. Not once. Nor had she thought of Jennie. It had never crossed her mind that Jennie might want to come to their wedding.

Sam and Katy arrive home just after five. "What's for supper?" Sam asks, tossing his jacket over a chair. A postcard slips from one of his pockets.

Liz picks it up. There's a photograph of Terri and Brian on

the front, the time and place of their wedding reception on the back. The photograph was taken at the cottage. Brian is looking straight at the camera—healthy, happy, strong. Terri stands by his side, her hair blowing across her face, looking up at him. Her expression suggests the picture was Brian's idea, that as soon as the camera clicks, she will turn and resume some wifely task.

Sam grabs the card from her hand. "I didn't want you to see that."

"It's all right Sam. I'm glad I did." In some strange way she would like to keep it. A talisman against all her hopes and fears.

Brian calls a couple of days later to say he and Terri have decided to bypass Chicago and drive straight to Edmonton. He's phoning from a motel. "Is Katy there?"

"I'll get her. Oh, by the way, your cheque hasn't arrived."

"We'll talk about it when I'm back. I spent a lot of money on new boots and riding pants for her."

"She didn't need them."

"She did need them. The separation agreement stipulates we'll share extra costs like camp, braces, riding clothes."

"Only if we agree to them." I don't believe this. He's on his honeymoon with Terri, fighting with me. She's probably listening. Just as I listened while he fought long distance with Helen. Tiptoeing around the room, stopping to massage the back of his neck, thinking, the poor guy, how does he deal with her? After he hung up, he'd turn and say, "Give me a hug." And she did.

"Brian, I need that money," she says now and hands the phone to Katy. She walks into the living room, glancing at her watch. Nine o'clock. There's a five hour difference between Toronto and London. It's four o'clock there. Helen is probably still at work. Is she lonely? Liz wonders. Does she still think about Brian occasionally, miss him? Wonder if there wasn't something she could have done to save their marriage?

Brian calls home every night or every second night to let Liz know where he is in case she needs to get in touch. In case the children want to call. It's as if he's away on a long business trip. Postcards arrive for the children daily. *We're having a good time. The scenery is beautiful. I wish you'd been with us today, Katy. We passed a field of wild horses.*

Did we send postcards to Jennie on our honeymoon, Liz wonders. Did Helen read them?

Brian calls the weekend they reach Edmonton to give her his office number. She writes it down, then hands the phone to Sam, home for the weekend. "It's your Dad." Sam is playing his new tape—Paul Simon's *Graceland*. The part about *losing love is like a window on your heart. Everyone knows you're blown apart. Everyone feels the wind blow.* Angrily, she switches it off.

Brian calls to let her know he's back in town and there's something he thinks she should know. She knows from his voice what he is going to say. "Terri's pregnant."

"Yes. You said it might happen and it did." As if that too is all her fault.

"Will that make me a grandmother?" she asks drily.

"That's not funny."

"When will you tell the children?" And Jennie. And Helen.

"I'll have to think about that."

Sam and Katy come into the room. "Who was that?" Katy asks. "Mum, what is it?"

"Your father will want to tell you."

"Terri's going to have a baby," Sam says.

"Oh how embarrassing," Katy says.

"He'll be fifty-seven when it's born," Sam calculates quickly.

"He'll be the oldest father in Canada," Katy says.

"Go and get dressed you two. We're going out to lunch. Someplace special."

She looks at her watch. Twelve-thirty. Five-thirty in London. Helen is probably on her way home from work.

Transitional Objects

"I have a collect call from Mr. Gibson. Will you accept charges?"

Before Caroline could answer, her brother Al cut in. "Carlie! How ya doin'?"

"Al?"

"Of course it's Al. Who'd you think it'd be?"

It was over five years since she'd seen him. The last she heard he was living in Florida. "Where are you?"

"At the Fort Erie race track. I'm comin' up for Mother's birthday."

Caroline has invited the family to celebrate her mother's eighty-fourth birthday. One of her sisters must have told him.

"How is she?" asks Al.

"She's fine. We moved her to a retirement home last weekend."

"I heard. How'd it go?"

"Fine. The movers cleaned out her apartment yesterday."

"This is a bad connection," Al says impatiently.

Caroline raises her voice. "It went fine. Just a few tag-ends to clear up. What are you doing at the Fort Erie?"

"Workin'. What d'ya think I'd be doin'?"

Drinking, she thinks.

"I'm comin' up on Saturday. Can you put me up for the night?"

"I guess so."

"What d'ya mean, I guess so. Can you put me up or not?"
"Of course."
"That's better. We'll get there around five."
"We?"
"Me and Amanda."
"Amanda?"
"My dog. I was wondering if I could leave her with you for a couple of weeks. There's this stupid rule at the track against dogs."

Caroline does not want a dog to look after. "How many weeks?"

"Six."

"Al …"

"She's no trouble. She'll just lie around the backyard. And listen Carlie, do me a favour, pick up something for Mother. Spend a hundred dollars."

"On what?"

"Whatever you think she'd like."

"Al …"

"I'll pay you when I get there. And Carlie, pick me up a mickey of vodka."

Damn, she thinks, hanging up the phone. Why doesn't he buy his own goddamn vodka? A dog—on top of the kids, the house, work, the party.

She unfolds the newspaper and turns to the Food Section to check the weekly specials. There'll be nineteen altogether, but—apart from Al—her sister Margaret's son will be the only adult male. Her father has been dead for over twenty years, her brother Jim nearly as long. Her sister Margaret widowed for ten years, she and Barb both divorced for over five.

She'd met Margaret and Barb at her mother's apartment after the movers left. Dark squares and ovals marked the walls where her mother's pictures had hung, a layer of dust defined the place where her bed had stood. The apartment looked so small.

"It's hard to believe all that stuff fitted in," Margaret said. Margaret the eldest, plump and pretty.

"It's really dreary, isn't it?" Barb, one year younger than Caroline, shared the highstrung Gibson look.

"Well, let's get to work," Margaret said, leading the way to their mother's storage cupboard.

The cupboard was crammed from floor to ceiling. They threw out an electric fan that didn't work, a broken step ladder, a couple of old t.v. tables. Then began to sort through boxes of birthday and Christmas gifts their mother, Flo, had never used.

Caroline was surprised at how upset she felt. There was no question of Flo living on her own again; she'd started hallucinating, a side effect of Parkinson's. Nocturnal hallucinations. Cats jumping on her bed. Her sister Fay, long dead, sitting at the foot of her bed, reading a magazine, waiting. "She was dressed all in white," Flo told Caroline. "With a white veil wrapped round her head."

Like a shroud, thought Caroline.

"Another night I woke and found your father asleep beside me, his face turned to the wall. Of course we weren't touching anywhere."

Of course not.

"Another time I found Barb's daughter, Florie, sulking in the curtains. She refused to come to bed, refused to lie down with me. 'All right,' I said, 'I'll sleep on the couch, you can have the bed.' But when I woke next morning, though I was on the couch, the bed was empty."

She told Caroline, Caroline told her sisters. "What if Florie had wanted her to go for a walk?"

Caroline looks back at the list she has made for the party. She can get the food and wine at the corner but she'll have to go downtown for Al's present. And sometime over the weekend do a bit of work. She opens her notebook and makes a list.

> *talk to Lisa about school*
> *review house rules with Ian and Eric*
> *go to the bank*

pick up some groceries
call Mother

And now this:

walk the dog
put water down for dog
buy dog food.

How much will that cost? She loves her job and the pay's good, but Tom's support payments are becoming more and more irregular, the children's expenses costlier and costlier. At times it feels as if she's forever cutting corners, doing without, saving for a rainy day.

Al does not arrive Saturday at five, or six, or even ten. The party is well underway Sunday afternoon when his pick-up truck pulls up in front of the house. He's wearing jeans, a faded blue shirt, cowboy hat and boots, and looks like an elderly, pink-faced, beer-bellied parody of an American hero. For a moment Caroline doesn't recognize him. But then he turns and looks at her, his eyes as blue as ever, in them the mix of sorrow and defiance that paralyzed all the Gibson men.

"Sorry, Carlie. A sick horse."

Amanda is a smallish black dog, with touches of tan at her throat and above her eyes, like eyebrows, giving her a curiously human look. Her belly extends in a wide curve to either side, her legs dwarfed and bowed by the weight. Her face a small, pointed triangle, set against a perfect circle, like a child's drawing of a black sheep.

"Is she pregnant?"

"She's not fat," Al says quickly. "Are you Amanda?"

Amanda wags her tail nervously, not taking her eyes off Caroline.

"How old is she?" That might explain it.

"Five years in July."

"Al, she's a young dog!"

The kids crowd around the truck, more interested in Amanda than Uncle Al, though some are meeting him for the first time. "Here Amanda. Here Amanda."

Margaret gives Al a hug. "Hey, this is hard," she laughs, patting his belly.

Al pretends not to hear. "Who's this little old grey haired lady? Haven't you ever heard of Grecian formula up here?" He hands Caroline a white plastic bag. "This is for Amanda. She should have one or two tins a day."

Caroline looks inside: a couple of tins of gourmet dog food and two one hundred dollar bills. "Al, you don't have to do that."

"I want to." He looks around. "Where's Mother?"

"Inside. She'll be glad to see you."

"Of course she'll be glad to see me."

Inside Flo is sitting on a rose velvet chair, sound asleep, surrounded by flowers and gifts—similar to the ones in the storage cupboard.

"Don't wake her," Al says, opening the first of a pack of beers he's brought with him, just in case. He pulls up a footstool and sits watching his mother until the intensity of his gaze wakens her.

"Oh it's you," says Flo sharply, noticing the beer in his hand.

Al gets to his feet and joins Caroline. "So how's the filmmaking going? Any calls from Hollywood?"

Caroline ignores this. "How's it look?" She is checking the buffet she has laid out for supper. Salads, dips, olives, smoked salmon, chicken, cold cuts, fruit, cheese.

"What's all that?"

"It's called a buffet."

"A buffet?" he says, as if she's lost her senses. "Why didn't you just send out for pizza?"

After supper Caroline suggests she and Al take Amanda for a walk in the park across the street. She wants Al to know she has no intention of letting Amanda lie around the backyard. She wants Amanda to know it's Al's idea she stay.

"What do you usually feed her?"

"She likes people food. I take her to the restaurant with me most nights."

"What do you mean people food? Scraps?"

"Hell no," laughs Al. "I order her a rash of bacon for breakfast. Maybe a hamburger for lunch. A chicken for supper."

"A whole chicken! Al, that's terrible."

"What's terrible? She loves it!"

"You're lucky she doesn't choke."

The other dogs in the park are purebred. Golden retrievers, French poodles, terriers, Great Danes. Their coats gleaming, their haunches lean. Their owners fit and immaculately dressed. Caroline is embarrassed by Amanda, by Al himself.

"Christ, I hate those dogs," he says.

"What a thing to say."

"I mean those damn French poodles."

"They're beautiful."

"You think so?"

"What's Amanda?"

"I dunno. Who cares."

Caroline guesses she is mostly border collie. A dog she usually likes. Kind domestic animals, not too big, not too small, with long silky fur. She reaches down and pats Amanda. Her coat feels like steel wool. "How often do you wash her?"

"I don't," Al laughs. "She goes out in the rain once in a while."

Al is the last to leave. Caroline has been looking forward to a few quiet moments alone before going up to bed, but almost immediately Amanda begins to howl. Caroline opens the door so the dog can see Al's pickup is gone, then leads her upstairs to her bedroom and closes the door so the noise won't wake the kids.

Her bedroom is a mess. Stuff from her mother's storage cupboard everywhere. A framed reproduction of The Blue Boy that hung in her parents' home forever. Candlesticks that belonged to her grandmother. A bookcase her father built, the only thing he ever built. A mirror from her parents' bedroom, assorted knick-knacks, some of her old college books.

Strange what her mother had kept. They'd found a collection of hats from the fifties, a set of dishes from the days they were given away as door prizes at the movies. "What shall we do with them?" Margaret asked.

"Chuck 'em," said Barb.

"We can't do that," Margaret said.

"You take them then."

Margaret held up a lace table cloth. "This is pretty."

"Take it," said Barb, pulling a pile of yellow newspapers from the top shelf. Front page coverage of the Kennedy assassination, photographs of Jackie all in black, a special edition called The Kennedy Years, a framed portrait of the President. "Oh God, I'd forgotten about that."

Flo had mourned Jack Kennedy as if her heart would break. She had not mourned their brother Jim who had killed himself two months earlier, drunk on a highway miles from home, taking the driver of the other car with him.

The term *transitional objects* pops into Caroline's head. She can't remember exactly what it means. Objects ... or persons ... onto which we project our feelings to......

Her thoughts are interrupted by a resounding thud. Amanda has collapsed on the floor next to her bed. "You're fat and dirty," Caroline tells her. "If I had Al's number I'd call and tell him to come and get you."

Amanda wags her tail but her eyes are watchful.

I must stop this, Caroline thinks. Amanda is not Al.

Al. She could count on her fingers the number of times she's seen him in the last thirty years. And every time because he wanted something—a place to stay, money, a favour. The kids and Barb, especially Barb, have always loved him; his deliberate redneck humour, his generosity. They accept the wounded, outrageous, irresponsible person he has become.

Well, she won't.

On her way home from work the next day, Caroline buys a bag of kibble for overweight dogs. She fills a bowl and places it on the floor next to Amanda's water bowl. Amanda looks at it, puzzled.

Caroline rattles the bowl impatiently. "It's dogfood, Amanda. It'll do you the world of good."

Amanda retreats under the kitchen table.

Sighing, Caroline rummages in the fridge for the utility chicken she's bought at the local super-market. She covers it with water, brings it to a boil, lets it simmer until it's tender, then pours the broth from the chicken into a jug and skims off the fat. When the broth is lukewarm—she tests it on her wrist the way she used to test baby formula—she pours it over the diet kibble.

Amanda waddles over to the bowl, sniffs, and begins to eat.

Caroline's daughter, Lisa, saunters into the kitchen.

"Look," says Caroline. "Amanda's eating her diet food!"

Lisa, now fifteen, is slender, and lovely. "Mum, you're the one who should be on a diet."

"How can I diet with so much on my mind?"

"Mu-um ..." Lisa begins, making it a two syllable word.

"I want you to help bathe her. She's filthy."

"Where?"

"In the bathtub, where do you suppose?"

Lisa holds Amanda's head while Caroline soaps and rinses her. The water runs brown. Caroline washes her a second time. She's about to do it a third time when Amanda jumps out of the tub and shakes, drenching Caroline from head to toe. Caroline laughs, exhilarated.

She phones her mother. "I was wet from head to toe."

"The poor dog," says Flo reproachfully. "Make sure she's dry before you let her out."

Amanda is lying with her head on Lisa's lap, looking at Caroline as if to say, What did I ever do to you?

Caroline gets up early so she can take Amanda for a walk before she leaves for work. As she steps out the door, a stationwagon pulls into the driveway she shares with her neighbour. The driver waves. It's

Tony the carpenter, a familiar figure on the block when they first moved in, when everybody was renovating. "Tony, I'm so glad to see you! It's been years."

"You look good," Tony beams. "Much better than the last time I saw you."

Caroline leans forward and adjusts Amanda's collar. Her coat feels wonderfully silky. "I feel fine." Thankful she's wearing a loose top over her sweat pants. She's grown thick around the middle. Tony is lean and hard, with scarcely a grey hair. She wonders if he knows about Grecian formula. Only his eyes—faded and smaller—seem to have aged.

"You gotta new dog?"

"I'm babysitting for my brother."

Tony pats Amanda. "She's too fat. Animals are like people, they need lotsa exercise."

"I'm taking her for a walk."

Tony glances at the house. "The house looks just the same."

"It hasn't changed much." She'd intended to make all sorts of changes after Tom left, but had never found the time.

"Call me if you need anything done."

"I will."

The park across the street is the size of a small city block, but there's a larger one a few blocks away, beyond the cemetery. Caroline turns in that direction, Amanda waddling beside her like an overweight matron.

The last time I saw you. The summer before Tom left, she'd called Tony to do a few things around the house—clean the fireplace, adjust a door, rewire a lamp. She liked to sit and watch him work. He could fix anything, build anything. Tony laughed when she complimented him. "It's my job, Mrs. McNally. But she could see he was proud of his work, he loved what he was doing. The house felt good with Tony in it.

Inside the park, Amanda pauses—her expression soulful, her haunches quivering. *Stoop and Scoop* a sign warns all who enter. Caroline pulls a plastic bag from her pocket.

At work Caroline pictures Amanda waiting at home, eager to see her. But not, she knows, as eager as she is to see Lisa. *I'm the one who walks her, but Lisa is the one she loves.* But then Lisa doesn't deprive her of chicken, and she suspects Lisa lets her up on her bed at night. Well, at least the dog is clean.

It dismays Caroline to think Al let Amanda sleep on his bed unbathed. She tries to imagine the two of them in California. Al has been married three times and has four children but now lives alone. In a house trailer, Amanda his only companion. She pictures them at the end of the day walking along a dusty road to the local restaurant. Does Amanda sit up at the counter next to him, she wonders, or lie under the table at his feet? Maybe he feeds her on the way home. She hopes so. She hopes he has that much judgment. That he doesn't drink his supper while Amanda eats hers.

At the party Margaret's daughter, a nurse, had whispered that Al's hard belly and pink cheeks could be signs of cirrhosis of the liver. Caroline can't bear the thought. Al was such a beautiful, golden-haired child. She'd worshiped him then. They'd vowed to live together when they grew up—like old Mr. Hopper and his sister across the street. Neither of them would ever marry. She would never be mean like their mother, he would never drink like their father.

One morning a few weeks later Caroline notices a workman removing the No Dogs Allowed sign at the entrance to the cemetery. "Does that mean dogs are allowed?" Caroline asks. "As long as they're on a leash, lady."

She keeps Amanda on her leash as long as they are in sight of the gatehouse, then sets her free. Amanda races ahead, nose to the ground, tail wagging, then flies off to chase a squirrel. Like a young dog, Caroline thinks, pleased. Amanda has been on her diet for several weeks now and the pounds are slowly dropping from either end. Her head and shoulders beginning to look quite elegant, her haunches lean. Only her belly resists change.

The cemetery is cool and quiet. No one around. Many of the older tombstones are sandstone, some so worn they're illegible. But not all. Caroline glances at the names—*Graham, Kilgour, Boyd, Robertson*— then stops to read the small print. *Jennie Boyd, born Jan. 25, 1836, died Oct. 12, 1857, aged 21 years.* From what? she wonders. T.B., the flu? *Hanna Porter, aged 30 years, 7 months, beloved wife of Samuel Porter.* Probably died in childbirth. *Sabella Ferguson too—beloved wife, aged 39, 1842.* Beneath Sabella's name, the names of her children: *Christina, 1831, 10 mos, George Sinclair, 1832, 3 days, Byron Alexander, 1842, 2 mos.* Were there other children, between George and Byron, children who lived?. Caroline hopes so.

Next to Sabella lies Mary Sweetapple, dead at 83, after a pure good life alone. A pure good life. Who thought so? Nearby is Margaret Swann, 1876, 90 years, *Relict of Francis Swann* who died in 1832. So some women survived their husbands even then. But they couldn't count on it. Children died, young men died, men and women died in their prime. Edwin Bell, aged 23. Charles Wiley, aged 38. Becky Tyrell at the age of 55. That must have seemed a good long life then.

Her mother was 55 when her father died. She's been a widow for almost thirty years. Living alone, collecting things, waiting for one of her children to call. Her father wasn't much older than Al is now when he died. Younger than Al when he stopped drinking. She wonders when Al's serious drinking started. Probably when he started to work on the horse farm. Some pretty heavy drinking went on there, she knows.

To this day she's never really understood Al's love of horses. His willingness to work as a stable boy, cleaning out the stalls, exercising the horses—anything to be near them. As a young man he spent all his spare time learning to ride and jump. Taking part in small fairs, then bigger ones, then finally the Royal Winter Fair. Everyone was thrilled when he won the jumping category. Dumbfounded when he was offered a job in New York. A big job, a job, as it turned out, he didn't have the confidence for. Maybe that was when the heavy drinking started.

Well, he never let his kids down. He looked after them when their mother left, taking whatever steady work he could get to support them—long distance trucker, nightwatchman. Only when they no longer needed him, when they had finished school, did he start working with horses again.

Caroline thinks of the photograph of Al that stood on an end table in her mother's apartment for so long. Al jumping at the Winter Fair. Young, lean, handsome in his riding habit. The Al she loved, the Al she hoped would redeem himself. As her father had. As Jim might have, she likes to think, if he'd lived longer. Caroline looks around at the tombstones, some shaped like crosses, others flat and rounded. Ostentatious marble pillars, interspersed with modest markers on the ground. Tall ones, short ones, thick ones, thin. Like the human race.

Amanda, she thinks suddenly. Where is she? I should have been watching. "Amanda! Amanda?" What have I done. "Here Amanda!" Oh God if I've lost her …

From behind a large tombstone, Amanda bounds up to her joyfully.

"Oh Amanda," Caroline croons with relief. "Good girl. Good girl Amanda." She kneels down to stroke her.

Amanda licks her cheek.

"Amanda looks beautiful," Margaret exclaims. "Wait till Al sees her."

"You should keep her." Flo says, reproachfully. "She's so happy with you."

Amanda is lying with her head on Caroline's lap. "I wish I could."

Barb is shocked. "Caroline, she's Al's dog! Why do you want to keep Al's dog?"

"He doesn't deserve her," Flo intervenes. "The way he treats her."

"He feeds her too much," Barb says evenly. "That's all. She's not an abused animal."

Flo is staying with Caroline. The sisters take turns having her for the weekend, to give her a break from the nursing home.

"When's Al coming to get her?" Margaret asks.
"Who knows. Six weeks are up tomorrow."
"Knowing Al, she could be here for months," Flo says.
"She won't mind, will you Amanda?" Margaret smiles.
Amanda wags her tail.

It's been a long day. Usually Caroline falls into a deep dreamless sleep almost as soon as her head hits the pillow, but tonight she tosses and turns. And when she does sleep, she dreams—not about Amanda or Al, or Jim, not even Tom. She dreams about Tony.

In her dream she's visiting him. Tony as he looked when she first knew him. They're sitting side by side in a small cottage—the sort of cottage Tony probably grew up in in Portugal: low ceilings, white plastered walls, handmade furniture. She's wearing something loose and comfortable and sits with her bare feet curled beneath her, smiling.

Tony moves closer and rests his hand on her lap. It feels good.

"Mum! it's after eight o'clock!" Lisa is standing by Caroline's bed, looking down at her. "Aren't you going to work?"

"Of course I am." Shaking off the memory of her dream, Caroline reaches for her robe. Amanda stretches on the rug beside her bed. It's a clear spring day, one of the first. Caroline decides not to bother with slippers. It pleases her to risk the feel of the cool hardwood floors under her feet, the texture of carpet on the stairs, the tiles in the kitchen. Amanda is right behind her.

She fills Amanda's dish, goes to the front door for the newspaper. There she suddenly remembers another part of her dream. Tony has followed her upstairs to hang the mirror from her mother's cupboard. "I've put a mark where the nail should go," she says, and they fell back on the bed.

Caroline laughs, then glances up and down the street. Tony's stationwagon is nowhere to be seen.

Two weeks later Al turns up on her doorstep. Amanda doesn't seem to recognize him at first, then begins to moan, jumping up to lick his face.

"Thatta girl," Al laughs, taking a step backward. "She's fat!" he says to Caroline. "What've you been feeding her?"

"You're not serious!"

Al nods toward his pick-up truck. "C'mon Amanda, c'mon Babe."

"Aren't you going to stay for coffee?" Caroline blurts. It's too quick.

"Sorry, Carlie, gotta feed them horses."

"But don't you want to know what I've been feeding her?"

"Carlie, I know how to feed her."

Amanda runs ahead to the pick-up truck and leaps into the cab. It's grimy with dust, littered with straw and stable gear. Amanda doesn't care. Her nose begins to quiver in pursuit of some more important scent.

Al backs the truck out. He pauses where Caroline stands watching. "Look, I really appreciate this," he says, changing gears.

Caroline could swear she smells chicken.

"We'll be in touch," he shouts over the noise of the motor, then speeds off down the street.

Amanda doesn't look back.

What was the use? Caroline asks the sudden void. What was the use, she asks herself, the park across the street, the sky. The park is empty, the trees perfectly still. They seem to be watching, waiting. For what?

She walks back to the house and sits on the porch stairs. I should make a grocery list, tidy up, she thinks. But she doesn't move. The house looms behind her like a living thing. One day her kids will be gone and she'll have to pack up everything in that house, get rid of most of it, and move into a small apartment like her mother.

Thank heavens she has her work. She must call the office and tell them she'll be late. She's made a few appointments. Retired people, people who have embarked on new careers. She'll enjoy talking to them, getting to know their stories.

But what about my story, what about me?

A faint breeze stirs the upper branches of the trees. She pulls her notebook from her pocket, turns to a fresh page, and writes:

lose weight
exercise
buy new clothes

Her closet is crammed with clothes she hasn't worn in years. She'll give them away. Fix up the house, starting with her bedroom.

paint walls
hang Blue Boy
hang mirror
reorganize cupboard
build shelves

She'll need Tony for that. She looks back at the page.

have hair cut and coloured?

She can decide that later.

Haunted Space

The sky is blue, the air unseasonably warm. A beautiful Monday morning in April. Liz is dressed for work, making French toast and bacon for breakfast. Katy's favourite. When it's ready, she scoops it onto a plate and places it before Katy.

Which Katy ignores. "People do not have babies at his age," she storms, having spent Sunday afternoon with Brian, Terri and Adam their new baby—living proof, for all her thirteen-year-old friends to see, that her grey-haired father is fucking his new young wife.

Liz waits for Katy to add, "Do you know how embarrassing this is?" How many times has she heard that? But Katy lapses into silence, her eyes angry, sad.

"Well," Liz searches for something comforting to say. "Pablo Casal's wife had a baby when he was in his nineties. Picasso was in his eighties when his last child was born." Katy is not impressed.

Adam was born in December. Liz knows her son Sam felt he had been replaced, but nevertheless he bought and wrapped a small toy to take to Brian and Terri's on Boxing Day. Liz had made Katy a list of suitable gifts for infant boys, had even offered to buy something for her. But no, Katy said she would buy her own gift. Then, minutes before Brian was to pick them up, she panicked, "I have nothing for Adam. I don't want to go." Sighing, Liz suggested Katy wrap one of the many stuffed animals Brian had given her over the years and take that with her. Katy went up to her room but came back down empty-handed; she couldn't bear to part with any of them, not one.

"Don't worry," Liz told her. "I'll talk to Brian. You can get Adam something after the holidays."

Liz is surprised at how little the thought of Baby Adam bothers her. Terri's pregnancy—the thought of Terri carrying Brian's child—had been intolerable. But who can resent a baby? A life? She even dreams of Adam from time to time. In one dream he spoke several languages, a brilliant child; in another he was already taller than any of them. She calculates now that in less than two weeks Adam will be four months old.

"I'm going to ask my Dad if Dominique can come up to the cottage this summer," Katy says.

Liz says nothing; the cottage is now Brian's territory, his lovenest. She knows Katy's new friend Dominique has a stepbrother about Adam's age. Perhaps that's what binds them. She has met Dominique just once: a tall, blond, startlingly cool girl.

"I don't want to be there alone with the three of them."

"Well, ask your Dad. Terri will be busy with Adam this summer." Liz spent fifteen summers at the cottage watching Sam and Katy grow. It outrages her still to think of Terri in her place.

"I don't think Terri likes it there." Katy says, reaching for her books. It's eight-fifteen.

Liz watches her leave for school, then pours herself a final cup of coffee.

The phone rings. "Mrs. Lord?" a woman asks.

"Well, yes." Liz has reverted to her maiden name.

"Katy's mother?"

"Yes. Yes, of course."

"Katy hasn't been at school for the past two months. Are you aware of that?"

"Of course I'm not aware of that. There must be some mistake."

"I'm afraid not. Mr. White, the vice-principal, would like to speak to you."

Thirty minutes later, a student ushers Liz into Mr. White's office. A tall thin man with rounded shoulders and a rueful smile rises to greet her. "Sorry to be the bearer of bad tidings, Mrs. Lord."

"Why wasn't I notified sooner?"

"There are twenty-six hundred students here."

That's no excuse, she thinks angrily. This is supposed to be one of the best schools in the city. "Katy leaves for school every morning at eight-fifteen and she's home by six."

"Where does she go every day? There's a poolhall down the block."

"A poolhall?" Liz perches on the arm of a chair near the door.

"The kids hang out experimenting with drugs."

Drugs?

"Do you know Dominique?"

Liz nods. "I was hoping Dominique would be good for her. That they would be good for each other."

"Mrs. Lord, Katy and Dominique are bad for each other. They're skipping together." Mr. White thumbs through the papers on his desk for a moment, as though wondering how much he should tell her, then looks up. "Dominique has problems of her own. Her father is dying of AIDS. She lives with her mother and stepfather during the week, weekends with her father and his lover."

Katy has told Liz nothing of this.

Mr. White watches Liz intently. "I think I know what you're going through. My son moved in with me a couple of months ago, his mother couldn't handle him. It's been a nightmare. He refuses to go to school, sleeps every day till noon, plays his music all night long."

The blind leading the blind, Liz thinks, easing into the chair. "I went through something like that with my son, the year my husband and I separated." Who knows how long it would have gone on if her mother hadn't offered to send Sam to boarding school. "He seems to be all right now."

"Congratulations."

Liz leans forward and places her purse firmly on the edge of his desk. "Mr. White, Katy's always been the good one, the one who gave me no trouble."

He shrugs. "Maybe she figures it's her turn. That happens."

She couldn't go through that again. The worry, the fights, the sleepless nights. She couldn't expect any more help from her mother. "What do you suggest I do?"

"I think you should get Katy out of here into a smaller school, away from the poolhall, away from Dominique. If she stays here, she'll fail her year. In another school, with some tutoring, she might still make it. There are a few months left." He picks up a sheet of paper from his desk and stands. "I asked my secretary to type up a list of schools you might look at." He points to the name at the top of the list. "This is my first choice. It's a small school in the east end. I know the principal. If you like, I could call him and put in a good word."

The school is a small grey building in a no-man's-land of marginal shops and dusty houses. In the schoolyard kids come and go in no discernible order; a group of boys stand smoking in the entrance. Why aren't they in class? Liz wonders. They turn and stare at her—her neat skirt and jacket, paisley scarf and well-polished shoes, her dark hair streaked with grey—unmistakably a parent, the enemy.

Liz tries to ignore her feelings, her feelings of antipathy to sixteen year olds in black leather jackets and torn jeans, the sharp sweet smell of marijuana.

Two boys hurry from the school, their voices high with excitement. "He should've been punished more."

"The guy's dead, man, how much more can he be punished?"

"They should've shot him up the ass."

Liz shudders. There is nothing here to stop Katy from skipping, nothing to hold her.

At home she dials Brian's number. "Brian's out of town for the week," Terri tells her. Great, Liz thinks, if there's trouble, I can deal with it. She calls her neighbour Caroline, who recently considered pulling her son Eric from the public system and enrolling him in a small private school. Caroline recommends

Durham Academy. "It's small, it's structured, and it's in the centre of town."

Katy arrives home promptly at six. Liz is waiting for her.
"How was your day?"
"Fine. The usual."
"The usual?"
"You know what I mean. What's for supper?" She opens the fridge door.
Angrily Liz moves Katy aside, closes the fridge door. "Were you and Dominique together?"
"Dominique's not in my class, you know that. What's got into you?"
"You were at the poolhall. You spend your days at the poolhall together."
"Who told you that?"
"Mr. White."
"Oh. I'm surprised he missed us." She turns. "I hate that school." And runs out of the room.
Liz calls after her, "I've made an appointment tomorrow morning at Durham Acadamy. We'll talk when you come down."
Upstairs a door slams.

Durham Academy is in an old family mansion, renovated and enlarged to make space for classrooms, lockers, gymnasiums. No crowded schoolyard to cross, the entrance immaculate. It feels safe. Safe and manageable.
The principal, Mr. Urquart, is a short, muscular man with a friendly, optimistic smile. He leads Liz and Katy into what must originally have been the den and now serves as his office. "Durham Academy is designed for kids who have fallen through the cracks of the public system," he tells Liz. If he has children of his own, he doesn't mention them. "Attendance and homework are monitored. There's a study hall. Extra tutoring can be arranged."
"What if Katy skips?"
"You will be notified instantly. But I'm sure that won't be

necessary." He smiles at Katy. "You're a bright girl, I can see that. I'm sure you will be successful here. All you have to do is attend classes." He smiles again. "And I'll make sure you do."

Liz can see Katy is impressed in spite of herself. But as soon as they leave the school, Katy smirks, "Do you think he's gay?"

"No, I don't," Liz snaps. "And what difference would it make anyway?"

They walk in silence to the subway. Katy leans against the wall and crosses her arms. "I'm not going to a place like that. You can't make me."

The heart of the matter.

"I want you to think about it, Katy."

"I hate it. It's preppy."

That night Liz tells Katy that she has thought about it, very carefully, and Katy is going.

"I hate you," Katy sobs. "You're ruining my life. I'll be glad when you're dead!"

She doesn't mean it, I know she doesn't mean it. "I understand that you're angry," Liz says as calmly as she can. "But you are going."

Katy rushes from the room.

Liz feels cold, her throat aches. She drags herself upstairs and crawls into bed, wondering if she is in fact dying. The same thought must have occurred to Katy, for when Liz asks her for a cup of broth and a thermometer, she doesn't argue. She lingers in the doorway while Liz takes her temperature.

"What is it? "

"A hundred and two."

Katy is alarmed. "You'd better go to the hospital."

"Dr. Young says a bit of fever's not a bad thing. It's nothing to worry about."

In fact it feels quite cosy, a good excuse to stay in bed. Let Katy worry about her for a change. She feels as if she's been trying to turn herself inside out since Brian left, to force herself through a keyhole, through the eye of a needle. On the other side, Caroline assures her, lies strength, peace of mind and happiness. "Maybe not the kind of happiness you dreamed of as a girl, but happiness. For Katy and Sam as well as yourself." Liz hopes she's right.

Brian suggests they meet in a self-service coffee house near his apartment. Mocha coffee in styrofoam cups, French pastries on cardboard plates. Liz asks for coffee and pulls a dollar bill from her purse.

Brian smiles, like a generous host. "Aren't you going to have a pastry?"

"Oh, is this a treat?" Liz hopes he hasn't noticed the dollar in her hand.

Brian stiffens, a man put upon, expected to give more than he intended. "If you wish."

Liz hands the cashier her dollar. In less than sixty seconds, she thinks, we've relived the entire course of our marriage.

She leads the way to a table and outlines what she considers the best options for Katy. A transfer to Durham Academy right away, summer at the cottage with Brian and Terri—without Dominique.

"Why not boarding school?" Brian says. "It worked well for Sam."

"Can you afford it?"

They both know the answer to that. Brian hasn't had a really big contract for several years. Not since the summer he designed the theatre for a California tycoon. That had seemed the beginning of a whole new life, the money and recognition Brian had always wanted.

Liz stirs her coffee. "Besides Katy's a different child. I really don't think she could handle it." She looks at Brian. "Durham Academy costs nine thousand a year, plus uniforms, and books and things. Of course we'd only pay half that amount for the remainder of the year. Plus a late registration fee and some tutoring charges," she adds briskly. "Can I count on your help?"

Brian is silent. "I have a lot of expenses right now."

He means Adam, she thinks, the cost of raising Adam. She

glances around the room. Two solitary customers are silhouetted against the window. An old man reading a book, a woman cradling a cup in both hands, as though for warmth.

"I'll pay half," Brian says finally. "But I'll have to get back to you about the cottage. I might not rent it this summer."

A possibility, in some ways, more final than divorce. "Have you mentioned this to the kids?"

"I"ll tell them when my decision's firm."

A door was closing. "But they've spent every summer of their lives at the cottage. Surely you can take it once more, so they'll know it's their last time...."

No reply.

She knows Terri doesn't like it there. "One last weekend so they can say goodbye to the place."

"I'm not sure it suits my plans."

"But you'll have to go up anyway, to collect your things."

"Not really," he says coolly. "There's nothing there of any value."

The address the school secretary has given Liz turns out to be a clothing shop. A men's clothing shop.

"There must be some mistake," Liz says.

Katy sighs theatrically. "I hope we haven't come all this way for nothing." She is wearing torn jeans, a black T-shirt and an old suede jacket of Brian's.

"Let's ask inside."

A clerk appears. A plump young woman dressed in a plaid skirt and blazer. "There's no mistake," she tells them cheerfully and leads them to the back of the store, to rows of plaid pleated skirts. Dark blue plaid, light blue plaid, green, grey, and maroon.

"Which school?" she asks Katy.

Katy crosses her arms and stares at the ceiling.

"Durham Academy," Liz says.

The clerk looks Katy up and down then takes a grey skirt and maroon blaser from a rack. She adds a white buttoned down shirt from a nearby counter, a grey tie, and grey knee socks. "You can try the oxfords later," she says, holding them out to Katy.

Katy doesn't move.

"You'd better try them on, Katy," Liz says.

"Why don't you try them on," Katy says evenly. "We're the same size."

"Katy...."

"Is something wrong?" The clerk looks embarrassed.

Katy glares at Liz, grabs the clothes, and disappears into a fitting room. She's back in minutes. "There, are you satisfied?" She places one foot awkwardly in front of the other, her arms hanging limply by her sides, her hair dishevelled, the collar of the shirt undone.

"Katy, you look wonderful, " Liz says. "The uniform really suits you."

"I am not wearing this on the street." Katy turns back into the fitting room. "I'd die if my friends saw me."

Liz calls through the door. "You can wear your jeans to school. And change when you get there."

Katy throws the box containing her uniform on the chair in the hall then runs upstairs to her room. Liz hears her door slam. The phone is ringing. It's Brian; he won't be renting the cottage for the summer.

"I can't afford it."

"I'll pay half," she says recklessly. She'll find the money somehow.

"I can't afford it and I don't want it. It's haunted space."

"Brian...."

He's hung up.

Liz breaks the news to Sam and Katy over dinner.

"I love the cottage," Katy storms. "More than this place, more than any place in the world. I'm never going to my Dad's again. I'm never going to wear that uniform, ever." She runs out of the room.

"Don't worry, Mum," Sam says. "She'll get over it."

Liz isn't so sure. She remembers how stunned Sam and Katy

were the day Brian told them they didn't own the cottage, they just rented it from Gord and Eleanor.

"Dad, why don't you buy it?" Sam pleaded.

"Because it's not for sale."

"Why not? Gord and Eleanor don't need it. They have a house."

Gord and Eleanor had built themselves a house closer to the road. "No, but it's always been in Eleanor's family. Her great Aunt Ethel owned it, then her mother.... She wants to keep it."

We made a mistake, Liz thinks now, investing so much of the children's lives in someone else's property. In the beginning they had intended to look around and buy something of their own, but had never been able to find anything they liked as much.

She dials Eleanor's number. It's the first time she's spoken to her since Terri took her place. Can she rent the cottage for a weekend before the season opens, so she can take the kids up to collect whatever they've left there? "Of course," Eleanor tells her. "Any weekend before June. But my dear, you don't have to rent it. Just come. As soon as you like."

The sooner the better, Liz thinks, before Katy starts her new school.

On the way to the cottage the countryside looks just as it did the day Brian told her about Terri, wiping out fifteen summers in one afternoon. Damn him, Liz thinks, I shouldn't have to do this.

The temperature is still unseasonably warm, the sky sunny. More like July than April. Sam has brought along his girlfriend. Liz has invited Caroline for moral support. Caroline is driving.

"There's the turnoff," Liz reminds her.

They coast through the valley, pull into the driveway, past Gord and Eleanor's bungalow, and there it is, exactly as Liz left it. A white frame house with dark green trim, surrounded by a wall of birch and maple and cedar, all perfectly reflected in a small, secluded lake. So quiet, so calm. Liz knows every corner of the house. Which stair creaks. Where the plaster continues to fall, no matter how often it's patched. The uneven pattern on the inside of the curtains. Exactly where the sofa sags, which tableleg wobbles. How the light changes as the sun moves from one end of the lake to the other. How it looks on rainy days, on starry nights. But it's the stillness, the spirit of the lake that holds her.

I love this place, she thinks. It has nothing to do with Brian and Terri. If there is a ghost, it's Joe. Joe, the family dog who died at the cottage the summer Katy turned eleven. Liz half expects to see him come bounding from behind the cottage to greet them, his tail wagging.

Caroline has begun to unload the car. "Where do I sleep?"

Liz hasn't thought about sleeping arrangements. She and Brian always slept in the front room, the room with the spool bed, the room overlooking the lake. She supposes that's where he and Terri slept.

"Where are you going to sleep? " she asks Sam, stalling for time.

"The room at the top of the stairs, if that's all right." Sam looks away. "That's the room Dad and Terri used."

"Well, in that case I'll sleep in the front room as usual. Caroline can have the room next to Katy's."

Sam turns to his girlfriend. "How about a swim?"

"Won't it be cold?"

"Who cares. C'mon Katy."

They race into the cottage to change. Liz and Caroline watch them go. "She's a perfect match for him," Caroline says.

It's true, Liz thinks. Sam's girlfriend is small and blonde, with masses of frizzy hair. Sam's hair is dark, his body compact and muscular. Like the men in her family. Katy's is long and slender, like Brian's.

Caroline sorts the food they brought with them. The kitchen's a big old-fashioned room, with a huge black stove, open shelves and casement windows. Liz opens the window that faces the lake. The sun has moved down to the far end, its light diffused by the willows that grow along the edge. She can hear the children screaming as they plunge into the water.

"I'll build a fire in the fireplace," she says. In early spring or late fall Brian always did that while she and the children swam. When they raced from the water, shivering with cold, he'd wrap each of them in a large warm towel, then lead them inside, where cups of hot chocolate were waiting for the children, a glass of brandy for Liz.

Over dinner Sam tells his girlfriend family stories. The time he stepped on a pitchfork and Brian rushed him to the hospital. The time a babysitter fell asleep in the sun and a playmate of Katy's almost drowned. The time Joe got caught on a barbed wire fence. Stories of peril and rescue.

Liz remembers happier times. Sam and Katy in their waterwings, splashing at the edge of the lake. Birthday parties in ascending order. Family walks across the valley.

"How old were you the first time you came here?" Sam's girlfriend asks.

"Six months."

Liz smiles. "Brian covered Sam's carry cot with mosquito netting and put him to sleep in the shade of the big maple at the corner of the house."

Sam smiles.

"Katy came directly from the hospital."

Katy does not smile.

"Lucky Katy. How did you find this place anyway? "

"Friends showed it to us." Led them along the crest of the hill overlooking the lake, the cottage. The view was so perfectly beautiful, so unexpected, it seemed like a mirage. They couldn't believe the cottage was for rent, they couldn't believe their luck.

The next morning Liz and Katy search through the cupboards. Brian and Terri have left no traces. Liz discovers an old baby blanket of Sam's, a sandal of Katy's about four inches long, a pair of cords Sam wore when he was a toddler. Katy finds a box of family slides, the dress she wore to her graduation from grade school, Joe's collar. Abandoned toys and books.

Silently, they stuff them into green plastic bags.

"Might as well put them in the car," Liz says, and leads the way. "There," she says, slamming the trunk door. "That's done."

Angrily, Katy turns and stares at the lake.

"Maybe Eleanor will let us rent the cottage for a weekend in the fall," Liz says cautiously.

"It won't be the same," Katy says. "Nothing is the same. Nothing." And walks off toward the dock.

Inside Caroline is peeling vegetables. "Liz, why don't you take a break while I make lunch. You've been working all morning."

"Maybe I will."

Liz steps out onto the front porch. The sun is directly overhead, brilliant, white. Liz closes her eyes, overwhelmed by a sense of the past. It's as if everyone who's ever been at the cottage is standing just beyond her line of vision, just around the corner—like actors in the wings, waiting to replay their roles. Her mother-in-law, babysitters, friends laden with food and wine, neighbours stopping to gossip, the vet who looked after Joe.

It's as if if Brian himself is about to join her. Any moment now the airport limousine that brought him back from California will come gliding down the lane and stop by the cottage. Brian will step out, handsome in a white suit and straw hat, and walk towards her, smiling. Bearing gifts for all of them. The driver right behind him carrying his bags like a trusted servant. She'll call, You look like the Great Gatsby, laughing as Joe bounds to meet him. Sam will look up from the book he's reading on the dock, as Katy comes streaking from the far end of the lake, hair streaming behind her, bare legs flying.

"Dad, Dad, what did you bring me?"

Liz wakes in the middle of the night to find Katy climbing into bed with her. As if none of it happened. The fights, the angry silences, the trouble at school. She looks so young. Eleven not thirteen. Katy, the good child.

"Mum, I'm scared. I heard something."

"It's just the noises of the house."

"It was more than that." Katy listens for a moment. "This cottage is owned, but not by Eleanor or anybody who rents it."

Liz smiles. "What do you mean, owned?"

"You remember. When Sam and I were little we heard Aunt Ethel's footsteps."

Eleanor's Aunt Ethel, the original owner, has been dead for fifty years.

"Katy...."

"We heard them. I know you didn't believe us, but we did. They started at the bottom of the stairs and stopped outside our door. When we looked, there was no one there. It was Aunt Ethel. I know it was. Who else could it have been?"

Liz pictures Aunt Ethel as Eleanor has described her—a tall, angular, grey-haired woman, striding through the valley to oversee the planting of trees, the same trees that now whisper outside their window.

"I believe in ghosts," Katy says.

Haunted space.

"I know you think that's silly."

"Who knows?" Liz looks at Katy. "One thing I do know, if there is a ghost, it's a friendly ghost, nothing to be afraid of."

Katy is very still, waiting for more.

Liz brushes the hair from Katy's eyes. "Aunt Ethel must surely love you, Katy, after all these years. She will remember you always. You and Sam."

And me, she thinks, and me.

"Time to go," Caroline says. "I'll turn the car around."

Sam is standing with his arms around his girlfriend, looking up at the cottage. Katy sits on the dock, looking out at the lake, Liz kneels to pull a few weeds from the lawn.

The horn honks. They climb in and the car drifts down the driveway, turning right along the valley road. In the rearview mirror Liz can see Katy huddled in the back seat, staring out the window. She tries to think of something to say, some words to make the leaving easier, but it's Caroline who breaks the silence.

"Well, back to the real world, back to the city, back to work."

Monday morning Katy sets off for Durham Academy in her jeans and Brian's suede jacket, her uniform concealed in an old tote bag.

She arrives home in the late afternoon wearing the uniform. Mr. Urquart had called her into his office and informed her that in future he would expect her to arrive at school properly dressed; no one is allowed into the building wearing jeans.

Katy is furious. "Can you believe that?"

Liz doesn't reply immediately. "Maybe's there's a restaurant nearby where you can change."

"Maybe."

But when Katy comes down for breakfast the next morning she is wearing her uniform. Liz can only assume she's decided that changing in public would be more embarrassing than being seen by her friends. Besides, the risk of that is small; Katy is now travelling in a different direction.

Or so Liz devoutly hopes.

Lonely Hearts

Caroline cuts through Allan Gardens. Three hundred and sixty degrees of light and shade, trees and grass, the park benches occupied by the same homeless men who will sleep there later. An image of Tom pops into her head. Sitting on the park bench across the street from their house, the day he came to take away his share of their belongings.

In the middle of the Gardens a speaker begins to harangue a group of unemployed men. "Christ came into the world to save the lazy, the unemployed. Not just sinners."

"Oh ya?" one of them shouts. "Feed the poor, He said."

The speaker shakes his head. "Get a job, He said, work."

Caroline knows Jo-Anne is waiting for her, but can't resist. She stops to listen.

A grey-haired man elbows his way through the crowd. "I tried to get a job," he says angrily. "Don't think I didn't. Don't think I like lying around all day." His belly protrudes over his trousers, his shirt gapes around his belly button. "Nobody will hire me. Nobody! You think Jesus wouldn't understand that?"

"Read the Bible," the speaker says. "There's your answer, in the Bible."

Caroline turns to the man next to her. "Ask him which chapter."

Jo-Anne is waiting outside the Carlton Cinema. "I got us tickets for 'Lonely Hearts'," she announces cheerfully.

"The Paul Cox film." Caroline would have preferred a comedy, something light. "It got great reviews."

The theatre is almost empty, the film has been running for weeks. The story of two flawed, lonely people who find each other—their grey lives illumined and redeemed by love.

As the credits roll, Jo-Anne wipes away a tear. Why didn't it work for Richard and me, that impulse to love and be loved?

Caroline gets to her feet. "What nonsense. I need a coffee. How about you?"

The waiter leads them to a table at the back of the restaurant, next to a party of middle-aged women. An expensively dressed blonde is holding court. "He couldn't get it in, he couldn't get it out. We flailed around for hours. By the time he left, my new bedspread was a mess, I was sore, and the day was wasted."

The others howl with laughter.

"Charming," says Caroline.

The laughter subsides. "Why don't we each borrow five thousand dollars from the bank," suggests another. "Go for broke, get a facelift, find a man."

"She's not serious?" Caroline says.

"Why not?" asks Jo-Anne.

"Because if it didn't work at 21 or 31 or 41, what makes her think it will work at 51 with a facelift?'

"I'm not 51 and I'm living the life of a nun." At night Jo-Anne lies in bed thinking, Dear God, let there be someone out there for me. Someone to grow old with. Someone to share my bed with. "I don't want to spend the rest of my life alone."

"There are worse things than being alone. In fact I've decided I quite like it. A relationship takes too much energy."

They sip their coffee in silence, then Jo-Anne asks, "What happened to … you know, the man at your party. He seemed nice."

"Handsome, charismatic, a drinker. Remind you of anyone? I attract … am attracted by … the wrong kind of men. I never seem to meet anyone who would enrich my life, or if I do, I don't notice. And I don't think that's ever going to change." She adds more sugar to her coffee. "What kind of man would you like?"

"A nice, undemanding, modest man." Like Richard.

"I know just the man. Should I give him your number?"

Alec sounds promising on the phone. Friendly, funny, a Glasgow brogue. An engineer from Scotland who's been separated for eight years. "When would you like to meet?" he asks Jo-Anne, adding in a tone that acknowledges their mutual predicament. "I'm free Saturdays."

"Saturday night's fine." Mark and Amy would be at Richard's.

"Good. I'll pick you up at seven. We can decide then what we want to do."

At two minutes to seven the doorbell rings. Jo-Anne has formed a mental picture of Alec—thin, wiry, with sandy hair and a roguish smile. Dressed in cords and a tweed jacket. The man on her doorstep is short and plump with grey hair, a small goatee and glasses. He's wearing grey flannels, a navy-blue blazer, a white shirt and tie. But the voice is the same, the smile warm, the eyes behind the glasses kind.

They decide on a movie. Which, Jo-Anne quickly realizes, is a mistake. Richard is a film buff. His ghost sits next to her, laughing at the funny parts, reaching for her hand in the sad parts.

"A good flick," Alec whispers, covering Jo-Anne's hand with his.

Jo-Anne freezes. "I'm sorry," she says. "This is my first date since my separation."

"I understand."

She wonders if he does, if he'll call again.

Alec rings the following Wednesday, inviting Jo-Anne to meet him at his local pub. It's a bit of a journey—Alec lives at the other end of town—but the pub is lively, the interior pleasant. Jo-Anne is glad she's come. She settles in for an evening of conversation and laughter. But within half an hour, Alec suggests they go round the corner to his place, so that Jo-Anne can meet his daughter and granddaughter who are staying with him.

A toddler runs to greet them at the door. Alec picks her up and puts her in Jo-Anne's arms. His daughter watches unsmiling. *My child is not a prop to entertain your latest lady,* her eyes seem to say.

With an apologetic smile, Jo-Anne hands the child to her mother, then turns to Alec. "Why don't you show me the house?"

A dreary house. The rooms small and dark, the furniture makeshift. And to make matters worse, within earshot of his daughter Alec begins to jump kisses on Jo-Anne, whispering, "Meet me for lunch tomorrow. Come to my office. It'll save time and that way I can introduce you to the chaps I work with."

Jo-Anne bridles. *Save who time?* "I'm very busy at the moment." she tells him. "I'll call you when I've more time."

And that, as far as she is concerned, is that. But Alec calls again a few days later. "Was it you who left a message on my answering service?" Jo-Anne can hear the lonely note in his voice. "No, it wasn't me," she says gently. Gently, but firmly.

"I've wasted two evenings," she tells Caroline. "That's enough." They're having a glass of wine in Caroline's backyard.

"Sorry. I should have warned you. He is needy."

Jo-Anne smiles. "Oh well."

"Why don't you put an ad in *The Star* or *The Globe*? Everybody's doing it."

"Oh, I don't think I'm ready for that." What would she say? *Reluctantly single fortyish woman—young fortyish woman, fit fortyish woman—happy in her work, her home, her children, badly misses the companionship of a nice....*

"Well, when you are ready, I'll help you."

"Did you write one?"

"I did. The year Tom left."

"How many replies did you get?"

"Eight. A married man from out of town. A cunnilinguist who wanted to share his enthusiasm. A manic-depressive. An ego-maniac who told me everything that was wrong with his first three wives. Who else? Oh yes, a mean little toad of a man who wanted to know right off if I would share the rent...."

Jo-Anne laughs. "Then why are you telling me to...."

"Because good things do happen. My wording was probably off. Besides you're younger. You look wonderful in green, did you know that? It brings out your eyes." She sips her wine. "Specify you're working in the arts. It sounds glamourous. Men like that."

"Trying to write is hardly part of the arts."

"Well, whatever you say, make sure it starts with A."

"What did yours say?"

"Forget mine. Listen to this. 'Artist wants someone to love, to share Mozart, to live with....'"

"Who wrote that?"

"A painter I know. That's how she met her husband."

"Sounds wonderful." But Jo-Anne isn't sure. Does she really want someone to live with? She can't imagine a strange man coming out of the bathroom, walking down the hall past the kids' doors into her bedroom. Someone other than Richard crawling into bed beside her. Someone else sitting in the kitchen, reading the paper, waiting for her to pour him a cup of coffee.

Still, the next morning she flips through the want-ads to Companions Wanted and there it is. *Artist, single male, semi-retired, mid-fifties, European background, fluent in English, French and German, interests include classical music, seeks sensitive, cultivated companion.*

Jo-Anne studied French and German at university, she and Richard spent a few months in Europe. The idea of an artist appeals to her. She cuts the ad from the paper and shows it to Caroline.

"I saw that," Caroline says. "Why don't you answer it. What have you got to lose?"

In reply Jo-Anne writes that she too is interested in the arts, speaks a little French and German, and loves classical music. She is looking for a supportive male, happy in his work, at peace with himself.

Another Richard. I must stop this, she thinks.

The newspaper stipulates that Friday is the last day replies are accepted. She decides to wait until Wednesday to mail hers. That way she won't know if it gets there in time; she doesn't want to spend the weekend waiting for the phone to ring.

"Mum, I'm starving," Mark complains. Jo-Anne tests the spaghetti.

"Hold on, it's almost ready." The phone rings; Jo-Anne reaches for it.

"Jo-Anne?" A male voice.

"Yes?"

"This is George. I got your letter." A deep male voice with a European accent.

"Mum, who is it?"

"Could you hold on a moment, please. I'll go to another phone." Jo-Anne tries to sound calm. "Mark, hang up when I tell you." She dashes upstairs to her room and grabs the extension. "Okay Mark." She waits for the click. "Hello again. Sorry about the confusion."

"That's quite all right." The voice is slow, throaty. Almost immediately it begins to question her: why is she looking for a companion. Is she single? How long has she been separated? What went wrong with her marriage?

Jo-Anne has no intention of discussing the break-up of her marriage with a perfect stranger. "I'm sorry, I'm in the middle of preparing dinner."

"Perhaps we could meet later for a drink."

"I'm sorry, I'm going out of town for the weekend."

"Oh." George sounds crestfallen.

Jo-Anne thinks, I really have no right to be this rude. After all, I did write him a letter. "Look, why don't you call me again on Monday about this time." He'll have forgotten all about me by Monday.

On Monday, at six sharp, the phone rings. This time the voice sounds familiar, almost like an old friend. "Could we meet this evening?"

The thought of meeting a stranger after dark makes Jo-Anne uncomfortable. "Tomorrow afternoon is possible."

"Are you familiar with Murray's at Bloor and Avenue Road?"

"Of course." Murray's, an old, established restaurant that sits like an anachromism in the heart of trendy Toronto. An interesting choice, she thinks.

"I'll meet you there ar four. I'll be wearing a grey suit and a grey shirt and, uh, a blue tie." George chuckles, amused by their little game. "My hair is grey and a bit thin on top. And, uh, I'll be reading a book. I'll sit at a table near the entrance."

What *do* I have to lose? Jo-Anne thinks, sailing through the revolving glass doors into Murray's. Her hair is freshly washed and brushed, her make-up flawless. As agreed she's wearing her green skirt and top, and carries a brand new purse. Inside she stops and looks around.

An old man, wearing a grey suit, a grey shirt and a blue tie, is sitting at a table near the window, reading a book. George. Oh no, she starts to back out before he sees her, but something inside her won't let it go at that. She steps forward. "George?"

George gets to his feet. His eyes are rheumy, his hands freckled with liver spots. He'll never see fifty again, or sixty. Perhaps not even seventy. Smiling, he pulls out a chair and motions to the waiter to bring Jo-Anne a glass of wine.

Quickly he outlines the salient facts of his life story. He is Hungarian. He brought his family to Canada in 1956 at the time of the Revolution. Before retirement he worked as a graphic artist. He has brought some pictures to show Jo-Anne. One of a beautiful chateau surrounded by an orchard. "That is where I grew up." Another of a heartbreakingly handsome man. "And this is me at age forty."

Jo-Anne would have loved him then.

"This is my wife at twenty. We were both students at the university."

Jo-Anne wonders how long she has been dead. Quite a while, she suspects.

"This is our son—he is an engineer working out west. And

this is our daughter. She's married and lives in New York."

"I guess you don't see much of them."

"No. I spend the summer months with my sister in London and each year I make a visit to Budapest. Otherwise I live by myself in a small apartment, where I paint small canvasses." He smiles ruefully. "I am occupied but I am lonely."

A courtly old man, Jo-Anne thinks. She would like to take him home to be her neighbour. She pictures him raking leaves in the yard next door. She pictures herself leaning over the fence, complimenting him on his garden, asking if there is anything she can pick up at the gardening centre for him. At Christmas she'll invite him over for a glass of sherry by the fire, encourage him to recount the story of his life.

Like Mr. Raoul, the old man who used to live next door. He too was alone, his wife dead. Over sherry he liked to talk about books or reminisce about the cigar factory he once owned, where he read Lorca aloud to the Spanish immigrants he employed to roll his cigars. "A tedious job." Now that he was retired, he liked to spend his days at the race track, although lately, he confessed, getting to and from the streetcar stop had become tiring. One afternoon he'd had to sit down and rest on someone's front lawn. The owner rushed out, yelling at him, thinking he was drunk. "Oh to be eighty again," Mr. Raoul quoted Stravinsky, smiling.

Occasionally he'd invite Jo-Anne over for a drink. "The house is just as my wife left it. I don't bother." He seemed quite content. But then a real estate agent, a young woman, persuaded him to rent her his second floor. His relatives, suspecting she was after his money—and who knows, perhaps she was—whisked him away to a retirement home. He died three months later.

George sighs. "I miss having someone who belongs to me."

Belongs to me. Jo-Anne knows what Caroline would say about that. "How many replies did you receive?"

"Seventy." He looks at her out of the corner of his eye. "You're my first choice." He studies his empty glass. "You're very young. I wouldn't make demands."

He means sexual demands, Jo-Anne thinks startled.

"I hope you're not the kind of woman who has, well, who has prejudices about age."

Jo-Anne chooses her words carefully. "I'm looking for someone my age, George."

She thinks of three elderly women who live in her neighbourhood. Bright, lively, charming widows. Any one of them a good companion for George. Should she try to arrange a meeting? Would he be insulted? Too risky, she decides. Besides, George has sixty-nine more replies to choose from. She has none.

"We parted outside Murray's. He shook my hand, walked a few steps, then stopped and looked back at me. 'How old do you think I look?'"

"What did you say," Caroline asks.

Jo-Anne smiles. "Sixty."

They're sitting on her front porch. A cat runs out from under the stairs, pauses as it catches sight of them, then darts nervously across the road, dodging an oncoming car. They watch until it is safely on the other side, then Caroline says. "You should place your own ad. That way you'd be in control. Or if you like, you, Liz and I could write one together. I wouldn't mind. Lots of women do that, then entertain the respondents over brunch."

Who would be in control then? Jo-Anne wonders. She recalls high school tea dances, the agony of waiting to be asked. "Maybe later," she says. "During the summer holidays, when Mark and Amy are with Richard. Or in the fall, after Amy's settled in high school."

"How about after Christmas," Caroline smiles. "Or sometime in the new year."

"If I a get a raise."

"Or when you retire."

They begin to laugh.

"Old lady wants someone to love," Caroline says. "To play euchre with, to go to church with...."

"To visit the doctor...."

"Walk in the park...."
"Sounds wonderful."

Family Pictures

On a large sheet of paper Liz has sketched three women relaxing on the shores of Georgian Bay. An image from her dream the night before. The woman in the foreground, plump and middle-aged, is wearing a house-dress, the kind her mother used to wear, but the curve of her body suggests a mermaid. She is smiling, and trails a fishing line in the water. Behind her, a woman wearing a large black hat, gazes happily toward the horizon. To the left, a younger leaner woman—in jeans and a T-shirt—sits reading.

My three selves, Liz thinks. No, Brian's three wives. I'm the one fishing, Helen's wearing the hat, and Terri's in jeans. Funny none of the children are with us.

She glances round her studio, which is set up in the bedroom she once shared with Brian. On the walls are paintings she's done of the children. Sam and Katy at the cottage, a watercolour of Jennie from memory. Jennie had called the night before to say she was flying over from London and Helen was coming with her. Something Helen hasn't done before, at least as long as Liz has known her—known of her—though Helen was raised in Toronto and her father lives here. "Grampa's sick," Jennie said. "Mum wants to see him. We'll go to his place from the airport, then I'll come to you. Tell Sam and Katy to be there."

Liz checks her watch. Eight o'clock. Sam and Katy are still asleep. She looks again at the sketch of the three women. "Paint seriously," her teacher has advised her. "Even if it's only on the weekends. Live with an image, let it grow." She's not sure she wants to live with this one. She takes it down, turns it to the wall, and goes downstairs for a cup of coffee.

It's September, her favourite time of the year, Saturday morning, her favourite time of the week. She carries her coffee out onto the deck, making a mental note to change the sheets in the spare bedroom—Jennie's room, Sam and Katy call it—and buy some flowers for it. How many times has Jennie made this trip?

She is filled with tenderness when she thinks of Jennie's first visit. Over twenty years ago, when she and Brian were first together, Jennie just eight years old. Helen had put her on a plane in London in the care of a stewardess, Brian went to the airport to meet her, while Liz waited at home, preparing dinner. When Jennie walked through the door she thought, She's so little, much too little for all this. But Jennie calmly pulled several notebooks from her schoolbag and handed them to Liz, as if she had come all the way for just this purpose. Books filled with pale pencil scribblings, drawings, additions and subtractions. Proof of her existence, her worth? Liz wondered. Or a peace offering to the wicked stepmother.

Jennie didn't let Liz out of sight all evening. She followed her from the hallway to the kitchen, from the kitchen to the dining room. And after dinner, when Brian announced he had some firecrackers to let off in the park, Jennie took her hand. Later, in the living room, while Brian played some children's records he'd bought specially for her, Jennie sat on the sofa next to Liz, and then finally put her head on her lap and fell asleep.

Smiling, Liz leans back and closes her eyes. It will be so good to see her. But she has mixed feelings about Helen coming to Toronto. She's pleased for Jennie—for once her three families will be in one place—but her own role as Jennie's stepmother seems suddenly redundant, her years with Brian reduced to a sort of interlude between Helen and Terri.

She has met Helen twice, both times in London. She doesn't like to think about the first time even now. When Brian and Helen separated, he decided to move back to Toronto, Helen opted to stay in London with Jennie. Simple as that. Or so Liz thought. Until it was time for Brian to settle the terms of his divorce from Helen, and he asked her to fly to London with him. She'd never been to London and looked forward to it.

But almost as soon as they checked into their hotel, the phone began to ring. Brian answered. "No," Brian said firmly. "This has nothing to do with Liz." It was Helen wanting to speak to her. "I'll call you after I've seen the lawyer. When? In the morning."

In the morning, shortly after Brian left, the phone rang. Liz knew she shouldn't answer but did. Helen sounded hostile, tearful. "Why did you come to London? This is my territory. What did I ever do to you?"

"Helen...."

"I'm coming over to talk to you."

"We can meet if you like," Liz said quickly. "But not here."

"Are you afraid I'll sully your love nest?"

"No," Liz said, as calmly and firmly as she could. "I just think it would be unnecessarily painful for both of us. Why don't we meet outside the National Art Gallery." No one would dare make a scene outside the National Art Gallery.

It was a cold, overcast day. Helen was waiting when Liz arrived. A striking woman, with enormous clear grey eyes, high cheekbones, and long dark hair tucked behind her ears. Dressed like an English schoolgirl in a tweed jacket and woolen skirt, a scarf thrown over her shoulders. Only then did Liz realize she had never once tried to imagine her, never once asked Brian to describe her, show her a picture.

"Helen?"

Helen turned. "Why did you do this to me?"

"It had nothing to do with you." Your life with Brian was over when I met him, she wanted to plead. Don't you understand that? Someone was bound to come along.

Tears began to trickle down Helen's cheeks, ashes dripped from her cigarette. She looked off to one side, her lip trembling.

"Helen, please, let's go inside."

Helen made no sign that she had heard. She took a deep

shaky breath, then looked down at the pavement and wept. People passing in and out of the gallery stopped and stared; an elderly man looked questioningly at Liz.

"Helen, please...." She should never have agreed to this.

After a few minutes, Helen threw her cigarette on the ground and stepped on it, fumbled in her purse for a handkerchief and wiped her eyes. She glanced briefly at the onlookers, then smiled ruefully at Liz, like someone conceding defeat. "You're prettier than I am," she said, then simply turned and walked away.

Liz panicked. She shouldn't be alone. Someone should be with her.

The second time she met Helen was the year Jennie turned fourteen. Liz suggested they fly to London for her birthday. Year after year Jennie had come out of the sky talking of her cat, her school, her bed, her garden. And Helen. "Brian, It's time time her two worlds met. It really is."

They took a taxi from the airport to Jennie's school, an ivy-covered stone building, where Jennie introduced Brian to her teacher. "This is my father," she said shyly. Her teacher said he was glad to meet him at last. Liz wondered how she would be introduced. "And this," Jennie said, "is my stepmother." So, Liz thought gratefully, I have a place in Jennie's life, even here.

Jennie led the way from her school to Helen's apartment, a garden apartment crammed with plants, books and cats. An upright piano stood in one corner, an old oak table by the window. It was here Helen poured tea. She had asked her friend Jake to join them. Jake, a short, balding man, was late. When he arrived Brian stood up—tall, lean and handsome—and shook his hand, then lapsed into silence. He and Helen said almost nothing the rest of the visit. Jake, a funny Irishman, tried to distract them with word games and funny stories. Without him the tension would have been unbearable: Brian still hostile, Helen still hurt. She loves him, Liz thought. After all these years, she still loves him.

The day Jennie and Helen fly from London, Sam and Katy hang

around the house all day, waiting. Sam spots Jennie's taxi the moment it pulls up in front of the house and rushes to greet her. "Oh it's so good to be here!" Jennie smiles, stepping into the house. She's wearing jeans and an old tweed jacket, a black scarf around her neck, her long hair untidy, her cheeks glowing. "How are you?" She slips out of the backpack she uses as a suitcase and gives Liz a hug.

"I'm fine," Liz says. "We're all fine."

Jennie turns to Katy. "You look wonderful. I like your hair."

Katy smiles, shyly pleased, instinctively fingering her new bangs. "How's your grandfather?"

"He's fine. Not sick at all. Just old and tired and lonely." Neither Katy or Sam know what to say to this.

"A cup of tea?" Sam offers.

"Of course I want a cup of tea," Jennie rummages in her backsack, smiles again. "I brought some oatbran cookies."

Sam leads the way to the kitchen. "How was your trip?"

"It was great. Great not to have to fly alone."

The next day Liz takes Jennie to lunch at the local bistro, a long, narrow restaurant with high wooden booths, a good place to talk. Jennie is full of news. A new job and a new lover, Angus. An evironmental lawyer, tall with red hair and a slow smile. "He plays the ukelele," she smiles, as if that clinched it.

"I'm sure I'll like him." Liz has liked all Jennie's boyfriends, those she has met. But it alarms her a little how quickly they disappear. "Do you ever see Toby?"

"Now and then. I bumped into him at a party just before I left. He looked great."

"I thought you two were a good pair."

"We were. But after a certain point I realized there wasn't going to be anything more than we already had. I wanted more." Jennie sips her wine. "He has a new friend. I think they're very happy together."

No regrets, no rancour. Brian and I will never achieve that, Liz thinks. She has learned to expect nothing from him but hostility. He has transferred all his love to Terri, just as years before he made the switch from Helen to Liz.

"I'm glad you're painting again," Jennie is saying. "It's what you were meant to do."

Liz laughs. "I hope you're right. It's the passion of my life at the moment. The only passion." She sips her wine. "How's your Mum?"

"She's fine. I think she's pleased to be here. Really pleased."

"Did you talk to Brian?"

"Yes. Sam and Katy and I are going to his place for dinner tonight."

After the children have left, Liz puts a log in the fireplace and pours herself a glass of wine, feeling restless: she's been looking forward to Jennie's visit, now here she is alone. Helen phones to speak to Jennie. Her voice as soft, as tentative as ever. Liz remembers Helen calling from London. The voice of a hurt child, she'd thought then, handing the phone to Brian. "What is it, Helen?" he'd ask impatiently.

"Helen," Liz says now, a note of belated apology in her voice. "You've just missed her. They've gone to their Dad's for dinner." Liz pictures Brian playing father to his three sets of children while Terri makes supper. "Why don't you call her there."

"Do you think it would be all right?"

"Of course it would be all right." It would be wonderful.

"Well, I suppose there's no reason why not."

"Of course not."

Liz waits until she figures Helen has said whatever she had to say, then dials Brian's number herself. Brian answers, sounding rattled. "What is it, Elizabeth?"

"I just wanted to let the kids know I'm going out for a while," she lies.

Three wives heard from, she thinks with childish satisfaction. Three wives present and accounted for.

"I'll give them that message," he says irritably.

Jennie is up before Liz. "I've made tea. Shall I pour you a cup?"

"Please. Did you get your mother's message?'

"Yes, I've called her. The Walters are getting together tonight."

The Walters. Helen's family. Jennie's grandfather, aunts and uncles and cousins. Liz knows them well. One reason Helen agreed to send Jennie to Toronto as often as she did was that she wanted Jennie to stay in touch with her relatives. Brian would invite them to Sunday dinner or weekends at the cottage. In a way they had gone on being his in-laws and become Liz's as well. When Brian left she received sympathy notes from Jennie's aunts and Mr. Walter phoned to say that she was still in their hearts and would always be part of the family. Now whenever the Walters got together Liz and the children were invited, Brian was not. But it's clear from Jennie's voice that Liz is not invited this time.

"Grampa said if Sam and Katy and I want to take a taxi, he'll pay for it." Jennie falters. "I hope you're not hurt. It's just, well Grampa thought it would be better if...."

"Jennie, I understand." Mr. Walter could hardly invite her to a party in Helen's honour. Yet people who know them both say they would have been friends had they met under different circumstances. Certainly they are alike in many ways. Both paint, both like cats, read the same authors, frequent second-hand stores.

"You know," Jennie says. "I sometimes think I'll get married if only to get you all together in one room. You, Mum, Brian and Terri."

This, thinks Liz, is ridiculous.

When Helen calls a few days later, Liz takes a deep breath and invites her to lunch. Jennie is enormously pleased.

"You make spinach soup and salad. I'll make bread. Mum is bringing cheese." She pulls a package of flour from the cupboard and reaches for a mixing bowl.

Liz washes the spinach, slices an onion and potato, adds chicken broth and nutmeg and puts it on to simmer. "Shall we eat outside? Or do you think it's too cold?"

"Not for Mum and me."

Liz fills a pan with warm, soapy water and goes outside to wash the table on the back deck. Impatiens and hibiscus plants everywhere. White, pink, orange and fuschia. A few golden leaves scattered on the deck. Helen will enjoy the colours, Liz is sure. Mr. Walter has shown her watercolours Helen did as a girl. And Helen's self-portrait, which Brian left behind, has wonderfully muted colours. She'd found it in the basement, stashed away with other memorabilia he no longer wanted.

She thinks of her own self-portrait, which Ron, a man she almost married, kept for years. When he finally returned it, she had absolutely no memory of painting it.

Liz goes back inside and puts a bottle of white wine in the fridge to cool, then hurries upstairs to have a shower and get dressed, wondering how much Helen has changed. It's fourteen years since she and Brian flew to London for Jennie's birthday. Brian was proud of her beauty then. She doubts anyone would call her beautiful now. Attractive maybe.

She pulls a blouse over her head. "You're getting to be quite grey!" Brian had remarked shortly before he left.

"Not as grey as you are," she'd laughed, thinking they were in it together. Liz glances over her shoulder at the mirror, half expecting to see Helen reflected there, smiling. *So Brian's left you for a younger woman.*

At exactly twelve noon Helen arrives for lunch. "My father sends his greetings," she says to Sam and Katy, her glance towards Liz veiled. Liz resists the urge to stare. Helen's slimmer than she remembers, her hair still dark—it must be tinted. She's wearing a flowered skirt and sleeveless top, her arms slender under the sweater she has draped around her shoulders. The soles of her sandals paperthin.

Liz is wearing Birkenstocks.

Jennie introduces Helen to Sam and Katy. Helen smiles. "I've seen pictures of you of course." She reaches into her bag for two small parcels, one for each of them. Small rubber stamps—a zebra for Katy, an elephant for Sam—with a printed note that says the proceeds from the sale of these items will be used to help save endangered species. "I couldn't resist them. They remind me of a stamp Jennie had when she was little. A monkey. She also had one with her name on it. For a while everywhere I looked

I'd find 'Jennie' stamped in red indelible ink. Even the toilet seat."

"Mum!" Jennie laughs.

"The landlord insisted we buy a new one when we moved, but we liked it, didn't we Jennie?"

Sam snickers, Katy smiles.

She's funny. Liz hadn't expected this.

"Mum, you sit here, next to Katy. Sam you sit there."

Helen turns to Katy. "Still taking piano lessons, Katy?"

Katy stopped playing the summer Brian left; there was nothing Liz could do or say to make her change her mind.

"No," Katy says. "I don't want any more lessons of any kind."

Helen turns to Sam. "How about you? Liking school any better."

"Not much."

"I can understand that," she says softly.

It surprises Liz that Helen knows so much about Sam and Katy, but of course she would, of course Jennie would tell her all about them.

"The soup is delicious," Helen says. "I don't have to ask who made the bread."

Liz smiles. "Whenever Jennie's here, the house is filled with the smell of bread baking. Scones. Muffins."

Katy objects. "Not just when Jennie's here."

"Katy makes wonderful cookies."

"Jennie taught me how," Katy tells Helen.

Using your recipes, Liz thinks.

"What about you?" Helen asks Sam.

"Sam makes the tea," Jennie says.

Liz remembers the wine in the fridge. "Would you like a glass of wine?"

"I'd better not."

"Wine puts Mum to sleep at lunchtime."

"It's true." Helen looks directly at Liz for the first time. Her eyes are not as luminous as Liz remembers, nor as large. But clear and present, no trace of malice in them. "How's Brian's baby? Has he changed much?"

"I've never seen him."

"You've never seen Adam? That's terrible."

Jennie reaches into her bag, pulls out three photographs, and hands them to Liz. "Here."

On top is a picture of a plump toddler, blond with big blue eyes—Terri's eyes—dressed in diapers and a baseball hat. So this is Adam. "He doesn't look at all like Brian."

"Not a bit," Helen agrees. "Not like these two."

Liz looks from Jennie to Katy. "They've got his eyes."

"His high tight bum," Helen says.

"Mum!"

In another photograph Adam is sitting on Sam's shoulders, squirming with delight. Sam is smiling, like a proud father. They're in a park somewhere, Liz doesn't recognize it. "Sam, you look like Adam's father."

"Do you think so?"

"Well, old enough to be Adam's father," Helen says.

Sam grins, pleased.

"Adam's crazy about Sam," Jennie says.

In the third picture Brian, Sam, Katy and Adam are sitting in Brian and Terri's apartment, on the leather sofa Brian took with him when he left. Brian is smiling—a bit eagerly for a man his age, Liz thinks—but Adam is bawling, straight at the camera. "My goodness, what was the matter with Adam?"

"He was mad because Terri made him sit on Dad's knee while she took the picture."

"Oh I see."

"Do you think Adam looks like me?" Katy asks.

"Maybe a little, around the nose."

"Perhaps the mouth," Helen says, then laughs. "Heavens, it's too soon to tell."

She is a pretty woman, Liz thinks. Prettier than she was fourteen years ago. More energy, more focus. She remembers how hurt Helen looked then. It occurs to her that maybe it wasn't love Helen wanted from Brian but recognition of their shared past.

She hands the pictures to Jennie. Jennie studies the one of Adam. "If I'm not married by the time I'm thirty," she says, "I'm going to have a baby on my own."

After lunch, after Sam and Katy leave for a movie with friends and Jennie goes inside to clean up, Liz and Helen sit talking about Helen's father, Mr. Walter. "He's just too old to make the trip to London anymore," Helen says. "I'll have to make the effort to come and see him from time to time."

"Jennie will like that."

Helen glances up at the house. "Your house is wonderful. A real family house."

"Untidy, you mean." Brian would hate that and they both know it.

"Well." Helen smiles.

Well, Liz thinks. Here we are, Brian's two ex-wives relaxing over a friendly cup of tea. "You're still working in the library?"

"Yes. And I've taken up pottery." Helen laughs. "I'm really quite pleased with my pots. Jennie tells me you're painting again."

"Yes. I seem to spend all my spare time at it."

"Good for you."

"How about you?"

Helen shakes her head.

"That's too bad." Should she mention the self-portrait? A moment of indecision. Then, "You know I have a self-portrait you left with Brian."

"Jennie told me about it."

"Would you like to see it?"

"I would actually."

In her studio, Liz sets Helen's self-portrait on her easel. Helen looks at it. "Oh, that's not mine. I didn't paint that, I'm sure I didn't."

Liz smiles. "I'm sure you did. It's been here all these years."

"But I have no memory of it whatsoever."

"It's very good."

Liz places her own self-portrait next to Helen's. "This is one

I did. I think it must have been about the same time. It was returned to me only recently."

"You did that? Oh, I like it. Wonderful colour!"

Liz laughs. "Like you I can't remember painting it."

Helen looks from one painting to the other then back at Liz. "What do you think that says about us?"

That evening, after the kids have left to meet Jennie's cousins, Liz rummages in the fridge for something to eat and finds a bit of Helen's cheese. She puts it on a slice of bread and pops it in the toaster oven.

We will be friends, she thinks. Helen will come to lunch whenever she's in town. We'll talk on the phone from time to time. Exchange notes about the children at Christmas.

More like family than friends really.

Harmony

Caroline had been about to leave for the library, to start research on a new film, when Jo-Anne called. "Come and have your fortune told. My treat."

Not Caroline's idea of a treat. "Jo-Anne, we're taking Liz out tonight, remember? Dinner and a lecture."

"Please. I don't want to go alone."

"How about after lunch."

"No. Better to avoid the rush."

"All right. But remember, you owe me one."

A few minutes later Jo-Anne stood on her doorstep, dressed all in black, blond hair tucked behind her ear, a fur hat pulled down over her forehead.

"You look like a Russian princess." Caroline was dressed comfortably in jeans and a baggy sweater, the kind of clothes she often wore to the library.

"Should I change?"

"Don't be silly, you look fine."

Caroline reached for her duffle coat. "This isn't about Richard by any chance?"

Jo-Anne looked sheepish. "We're thinking of getting back together."

"Maybe you should see a therapist, not a tea-cup reader," Caroline quipped, leading the way to her car. "Where is this place?"

The tea-room is in the east end of town, part of that no-man's land of marginal shops and dusty houses Liz visited years earlier, hoping to find a school for Katy. Caroline parks the car, Jo-Anne leads the way inside.

"You can sure tell who's serious and who isn't," Caroline says, slipping out of her coat.

Three tables are occupied by solitary, middle-aged women—one Chinese, one East Indian, one very WASP. All stare forlornly at teacups turned upside down on saucers. Towards the back, two young women giggle about the last time they had their fortunes told. "She told me I was going to meet a stranger with red hair. She tells everyone they're going to meet a man with red hair, she's famous for it."

One of a trio of young men at the next table leans over and asks, "And did you?"

The young woman smiles flirtatiously, "Well, not exactly. But someone in my office has red hair."

"Someone in most offices has red hair," Caroline comments dryly.

Just then an entire family enters, in the grips of mourning from the look of it. Caroline checks her watch. Eleven o'clock and the place is filling up.

She glances around the room. Sleazy curtains, rickety tables, dirty yellow walls decorated with plastic flowers. A sign warning patrons that what they hear within these walls is meant as entertainment only—it is not to be taken seriously. "This is the tackiest room I've ever seen."

Jo-Anne grins. "That's part of it."

A distinguished man with collar-length grey hair and a flowing mustache appears in the entrance to a corridor of booths at the rear of the tearoom. He is sporting a navy-blue blazer, grey flannels and a maroon striped cravat.

"That's John," Jo-Anne whispers. The man they've come to see.

"Number eleven?" John calls.

The Chinese woman gets to her feet—shyly, like a patient in

a doctor's office—and follows him.

Wordlessly, an old woman puts two cups of tea and a plate of cookies in front of Jo-Anne and Caroline, then gives each of them a number. Jo-Anne is number fourteen, Caroline fifteen. Numbers one to ten, Jo-Anne explains, are waiting for the woman who foretells red-haired strangers. "She's not in yet. Drink your tea then turn your cup upside down and turn it around three times."

"You don't have to tell me what to do," Caroline says. "My mother used to tell fortunes."

"Really! Why'd she stop?"

"Lost interest I guess." Her mother stopped telling fortunes about the same time her father stopped drinking.

John reappears with the Chinese woman, who thanks him tearfully, then—glowing with newfound hope—makes her way to the door.

"She was in there about ten minutes," Caroline says. "That means we'll probably be here about an hour."

"Number twelve?" The WASP woman puts down her book.

Jo-Anne reaches for a copy of *The New Age Messenger*—available free of charge—and hands it to Caroline. "Have a look?"

Caroline leafs through it, amazed at how much is going on. Lectures, seminars, workshops. Courses in basic crystal work, moon ceremonies for women, serpent fire for men, advice on how to heal a new age hangover for everybody. Even a Companions Wanted column for the psychically inclined.

When her turn comes, Jo-Anne gets to her feet with a grin and disappears after John.

Caroline goes back to reading. She glances up, aware someone is watching her. It's the Indian woman. "Your friend's been in there a long time," she says in a concerned way.

"Really?" Caroline looks at her watch. Twenty minutes. It doesn't surprise her. Jo-Anne must be a real treat after those other sorrowful women.

Another ten minutes have passed before Jo-Anne finally reappears, smiling. "Everything's going to be fine," she says to

Caroline. "I'll tell you about it later."

John ducks downstairs, presumably to take a pee, then calls Caroline's number. He looks her over carefully and concludes, "There's a dead marriage in your recent past."

Anybody could guess that, thinks Caroline.

"And a resentful daughter," he adds. "How many daughters do you have?"

"Just the one."

"Well, she's very resentful. You try your best to talk her out of it. Maybe you should back off a bit."

Maybe you should be a therapist, not a teacup reader, Caroline thinks.

"I see a man in your cup but that's not clear. You may marry again, but that's not central to your life. You're very independent. Capable."

In other words, I don't look like a Russian princess.

Caroline is beginning to feel quite annoyed. She's come for a teacup reading, not a character assessment. The kind of fortune her mother used to tell. Long trip, sudden inheritance, tall mysterious stranger.

"What kind of work do you do," John asks.

That's cheating, Caroline thinks, but tells him. "I'm a film-maker."

John raises his eyebrows questioningly.

"I just drifted into it. Like most women. The opportunity was there so I took it."

He looks back at her cup. "Well, no trouble there. Work and money will be all right." He pauses, then adds, "Yonge and Davenport will be important in your life. Does that make sense?"

Yonge and Davenport. Caroline pictures the intersection—Masonic Lodge on one corner, Canadian Tire on another, traffic zooming by. "I hope not."

John takes his cue from Caroline. "I also see a villa overlooking the Mediterranean. Does that make sense?"

Caroline suppresses a smile. "Certainly sounds better."

"You could attract a younger man." John pauses then asks if

there's anything Caroline is worried about.

"Like what?"

"A health issue perhaps?"

Caroline is startled. "Should I be?"

"You should pay more attention to your health, you really should. Exercise more, lose a little weight."

John puts down her cup and gets to his feet, signalling the interview is over.

Caroline glances at her watch. She's been in there five minutes.

The entrance to the church buzzes with excitement. Women greet each other—confident, happy. Women in their forties and fifties. A few men among them, but not many. Caroline recognizes some well known feminists, a famous painter, a novelist, an actress. Liz stops to talk to a few friends from her Sunday morning life-drawing class.

"We'd better take our seats," Jo-Anne says.

"Downstairs is completely full."

"Let's try the balcony."

Jo-Anne leads the way. The lecture is being held in St. Paul's Trinity Church, a church not unlike the People's Church of her childhood. Same period, same stone, although the proportions are more graceful, the pews fitted with red cushions—a concession to worldly comfort the People's Church would never have made. The whole brightly lit, like a moviehouse after the movie has ended.

A woman walks to the centre of the altar and turns to face them. She is wearing an elegant silk kimona decorated with peacocks, her dark hair loose to her shoulders, her manner unassuming. This is Dr. Alvino. The audience breaks into applause. Dr. Alvino is a well-known Jungian feminist, the author of several books.

"Thank you. Thank you very much."

Someone shouts, "You look terrific!"

Dr. Alvino calls back, "You look pretty good yourselves." The women clap and cheer.

This is wonderful, Liz thinks. It's her fiftieth birthday. Caroline and Jo-Anne have treated her to a wonderful dinner and now this. "The perfect way to start the second half of your life," said Caroline. Liz had been dreading turning fifty, the end of her forties, but suddenly it's all right. She has a whole new decade ahead of her. Fifty, fifty-one, fifty-two, fifty-three....

Dr. Alvino tells them she has just returned from a trip to meet the Dalai Lama. One of the spiritual highlights of her life. Since then she's been been mulling over the legend of the Holy Grail, the search for meaning in our lives. "What gives our lives meaning? What gives us a sense of completion, harmony, joy?"

Liz wonders if Dr. Alvino is married, and if so, what her husband thought about her going off to meet the Dalai Lama. Brian would never have allowed it. Well, that was then.

What gives her life meaning now? Her children, of course. Katy is doing well in school, Sam is at university. Her children, family, friends. And increasingly, painting. She's had her first show. A modest show in a small local gallery owned by a friend of her teacher. It was his idea, she didn't feel ready. Nonsense, he told her. I'll show you how to frame your paintings.

She'd worked for days. It was like getting the children ready for a birthday party. You look very nice dear, but I think you need a little colour here, a line there. Caroline and Jo-Anne had helped with titles, her teacher supervised the hanging. When it was all in place, she was surprised by its strength, its coherence. Four paintings sold—three to friends, one to a stranger. *Figures In A Misty Landscape. Animus/Anima,* Caroline called it. A member of the Jungian Society bought it.

Rick had posed for the male figure in the misty landscape. The first time she saw him she felt he'd stepped out of her unconscious. A dark young man, masculine but not muscular, strong but not aggressive. He modelled now and then for the Sunday morning life class, every gesture a study in mood and motion. A painter himself, he knew what worked and what didn't. Drawing him was like drawing part of herself.

She has begun to paint with a man she's known for years. No

danger of falling in love, they know each other too well. He's been through two marriages; his duvet, he told her, is all the relationship he can handle right now. She smiles remembering.

Dr. Alvino is speaking about harmony. Which, she says, should not be confused with pleasure. "When you suffer deeply, if what you feel is consistent with what you have just experienced, that too is harmony."

Liz doesn't like to think about how much she suffered when Brian left. In retrospect it seems like madness. There have been times since when she felt as if she'd lived a dozen lives and was just too tired to start another. But increasingly she has a direct sense of the world and her place in it.

"We all face difficulties, we all experience pain." Dr. Alvino pauses to give them time to think about this.

Liz becomes aware of Caroline moving restlessly beside her and wonders what she's thinking about. Her work? Her children?

Dr. Alvino returns to the theme of the Holy Grail. The chalice Christ held at the Last Supper, the chalice He filled with wine, saying, this is my blood. Dr. Alvino smiles. "Now a chalice filled with blood is a very feminine symbol, a sacred feminine symbol. The womb filled with menstrual blood."

Jo-Anne thinks how horrifed her mother would be to hear Jesus—her Jesus, her Saviour—mentioned in the same breath as menstrual blood.

"How mysterious—and magical—menstruation must have seemed to men before they understood the link between conception and birth," Dr. Alvino continues. "The onset of monthly bleeding at puberty, its disappearance during pregnancy and again at menopause with the coming of wisdom."

Jo-Anne has never heard menstruation, let alone menopause, mentioned in church before. The virgin birth yes, but monthly bleeding—never. She thinks of all the times she sat or knelt in church feeling like an outsider, an onlooker at a male feast hoping for a handout, a sinner hoping to be saved. Now, for the first time, she feels central, she feels sacred. Something closed has opened, a stone has rolled away.

Suddenly the air is filled with music. Recorded electronic, new-age music. Oh dear, Caroline thinks, trying vainly to hold on to her sense of the moment.

Dr. Alvino asks them to close their eyes and think back to when they were children. Joyful, innocent, trusting, playful children. In a beautiful, green and sacred place. Think back to a time when they felt loved and safe.

Caroline feels like she did in school when asked to write an essay about her summer vacation. She never had a summer vacation, not in the sense they meant. Now she can't think of a single time when she felt loved and safe. When she was a child, before her father stopped drinking. Not one. Maybe it's the way her memory works, storing up the bad times, letting the good times go. There are long periods she can't remember at all. Maybe she'd been perfectly happy then. She looks at the heads bowed around her and thinks back to all the houses she lived in as a kid. The nights she lay awake listening to her parents fight. She wants to weep. For all of them, her mother, her father, her brothers Al and Jim, her sister Barb.

She forces herself to try and remember the good times. The year they moved to Woodhill Crescent and she had a room of her own. But she was thirteen then, not a child. Evenings when the family sat around the kitchen table, singing.

Singing. Usually Christmases were really bad. Her father's binges always began at Christmas. But one year when her father had disappeared and there wasn't any money at all, Jim had led Al, Barb and her around the neighbourhood singing carols. Christmas Eve. Jim couldn't manage both his crutches and the guitar, so Al carried the guitar as they trudged from door to door, then handed it to him at the last moment.

Silent night, holy night, All is calm, all is bright, they sang in three part harmony.

Who could resist a caroller on crutches? They made a fortune. And at the very last minute rushed to the five-and-dime before it closed. Everything was on sale. Caroline still remembers the bright blue fur mitts she bought for her new baby sister, the beautiful china cup and saucer she bought for her mother.

A happy memory, but would Dr. Alvino consider it *safe* and *loved*? Caroline thought not.

Everyone is quiet on the way home. Was I the only one to fail that inward journey, Caroline wonders. She glances at Liz and Jo-Anne. Well, I feel it now, she thinks. I feel safe and loved now.

She drives down Constitution Avenue then turns left onto their street. It's after ten, the corner store in darkness, but lights burn brightly on their block. She pulls up in front of Liz's home.

Liz searches for her keys. "Would you like to come in for a glass of wine?"

"Richard is waiting for me," Jo-Anne says. "We've got things to talk about."

"And I've got to feed the dog," Caroline says.

The cat is waiting by the gate to greet Liz. Inside the house is quiet; Katy has gone to bed, leaving a note on the hall table. *Your mother called, and Sam.* Katy's books are strewn across the dining room table, and she's left the light by the piano burning. As far as Liz knows, this is the first time Katy has touched the piano since Brian left. She looks to see what Katy was playing. The Mozart sonata.

She pours herself a glass of wine, turns out the lights, and steps outside onto the front porch. She sips her wine and hums the Mozart sonata. Music she bought months ago, hoping to tempt Katy to play again. She phoned Katy's teacher, then phoned the music store to make sure they had it. But when she got there, she couldn't remember the number.

"You phoned a while ago, didn't you?" A young clerk leapt to his feet, dark eyes flashing like a younger, leaner Pavarotti. "It was Kershel 545. Here it is." He reached for the music, then began to sing. *Pum pum pum, pum de um dum dum.*

"No, that's not it." Liz hesistated, then hummed the melody that had been running around in her head all day. He joined her singing.

"That's the middle movement," he said, opening the music with a flourish. "There, you see."

It was wonderful. Like speaking another language. Liz didn't bother to tell him she couldn't read music.

She glances across the street at the park. It's a beautiful, clear, moonlit night. The shadows long but not threatening. A few stragglers walk their dogs, a neighbour stops to wave.